Look Into the Mirror

A Stephen Blackman Mystery

D.G. Stern

NEPTUNE PRESS

NEPTUNE PRESS

WWW.NEPTUNEPRESS.ORG

Printed in the U.S.A.

Publisher's Cataloging-In-Publication Data

Names:
Stern, D. G., author.
Title:
Look into the mirror / D.G. Stern.
Description:
[Orlando, Florida], Neptune Press, [2023] | Series: A Stephen Blackman mystery
Identifiers:
ISBN: 978-0-9906103-8-0 | LCCN: 2023944948
Subjects:
LCSH: Private investigators--Fiction. | Twins--Fiction. | Brothers--Fiction. | False personation--Fiction. | Attempted murder--Fiction. | Murder--Investigation--Fiction. | LCGFT: Detective and mystery fiction.
Classification:
LCC: PS3619.T477 L66 2023 | DDC: 816/.3--dc23

Magic mirror on the wall, who now is the fairest one of all?

— *The Queen in Snow White*

CHAPTER ONE

She sounded upset—demanding on the phone—insistent. It's really none of her business. Nothing is going to be accomplished by her interference. Certainly, nothing good. The expression "no good deed goes unpunished," sadly, has added meaning.

There are so many things that can go wrong in the blink of an eye. Actually, there are also many things that can go right during the same brief period. However, it is usually the former which we experience far too often.

One can always tell when it's going to be one of those days. Maybe it's the Florida weather—gray, damp, and humid, rapidly heading into a dark, wet, and clammy night. It might also be the tone in her voice when she insists they meet—right away. Her usual upbeat, staccato way of speaking gives way to a slow, deliberate, angry delivery. Damn it, he thinks, it shouldn't have to come down to this.

Things are not tropically warm and breezy for Ryan McCallum as he enters the gated, palm tree lined neighborhood of expensive homes, each of which rests on perfectly manicured lawns with its own pool. This is where Margaret lives. For some reason it reminds Ryan of an earlier, pre-divorce life. It seems so much in the distant past, but in reality it was only four years ago.

Four years ago

It seems like yesterday when a thirty-five-year-old woman with a master's degree in English, but absolutely no office skills, applied for a job. When did the office assistant become the executive assistant, and then vice president of communications? And more importantly, when did the hard-working employee become a friend—that's not fair— his best friend. How could it possibly be coming down to this? It's not right. There have to be boundaries which must be respected. She just doesn't understand.

Actually, she does understand most everything, only too well, but not this problem. She can't comprehend how he feels. The conflict and the pain. It's wrong of her to be judgmental. It's not a matter of black and white. She is simplifying everything, but everything is far from simple. Somehow, some way, he has got to get that through to her. Clarity and focus—it's a matter of life and death.

The windshield wiper on the silver Mercedes S 560 Coupe crosses the wide expanse. It really is a classy neigh-borhood, provided you appreciate gobs of green; literally and figuratively. Ryan prefers the 24/7 life that the city offers. Maybe that's why they haven't moved in together. Or is it?

She needs her garden, her pool, her escape, while he needs continuous stimuli. Her flowers bring her peace, comfort, and a stabilizing force that levels her highs and lows. She considers her garden a metaphor for life itself, bringing new hope each spring.

Why does this have to come between them? Everything was terrific. At least, that's what he thought. The company is flourishing; they have plenty of money; they travel to interesting places; attend cultural, social, and charitable events. They have it all. They are a couple in the best sense of the word. Why this? Why now?

The silver sedan turns into the driveway at number 3429 Hibiscus Lane and slowly rolls to a stop on the loose gravel. The houses, the swaying trees, and the people—the essence of a neighborhood—are all shrouded by the encroaching darkness. He hesitates momentarily. Ryan would much rather listen to Vivaldi's *Four Seasons* on the CD player than confront Margaret.

You can only prolong the inevitable for so long. After about five minutes idling in front of the attached three-car garage, silencing the purring engine, Ryan unbuckles his seatbelt and quickly glances into the rear-view mirror and his own sad eyes stare back at him. A window into his soul?

As he opens the heavy car door, an involuntary shiver runs down his spine. It can't be the coldness of the evening, it's still almost 80-degrees outside. It is the heaviness in his heart. He is positive that Margaret has been watching him from behind the curtained window, although he has seen neither her silhouette nor her shadow. He just knows. He feels her presence, and it is like ice.

The bounce is gone from his step and is replaced by a surface shuffle that makes him appear closer to seventy than his athletic forty-four years. He follows the path bordered by tiny glowing lights which makes everything look like Disney World. But this is not going to be fun. Anything *but* fun. He is weighted down with certain information, which really shouldn't be his burden—exactly.

The stillness in the air is suffocating, crushing his spirit with each painful step.

The doorbell's chime echoes off the marble foyer. Ryan's mind momentarily wanders. Margaret always had exquisite taste. Perhaps, he should give up the constant demands of corporate America, abandon the urban landscape, and settle down into a more pastoral life. Suddenly, his musings are interrupted as the door opens. It's probably too late anyway.

"Come in, Ryan." Margaret's voice is higher pitched than her 5'10" frame would suggest. She certainly didn't dress for the occasion. Her jeans show mud stains where she has undoubtedly been kneeling to tend to her precious plants. Margaret's long blond hair is tied with a simple ribbon and falls down the nape of her neck. There is nothing she can do to obscure her beauty. She is drop-dead gorgeous. *Christ —why is this happening?*

"Thanks." Ryan crosses the threshold, stepping defensively into *her world*. Over the years, Ryan McCallum has perfected the art of securing home field advantage, that edge over an opponent in a negotiation, albeit slight. If he couldn't control the actual place, he scouted the location, almost like a Presidential Advance Agent. Ryan made a point of always researching his adversary–looking for weaknesses.

He recalls that during a protracted—and increasingly difficult—meeting in Tokyo, which was being conducted in both Japanese and English because the CEO of the electronic manufacturing concern wanted everything translated for *clarity's sake*. Never one who suffers a fool, Ryan lost his temper. He told the corporate executive that he didn't have time to screw around. The Japanese CEO took great offense, threatening to leave the meeting and end discussions. Ryan simply slid a single piece of paper across the table. The CEO looked down, then up at Ryan, then down at the paper. He began to laugh. "Touché," he said. The paper was a photocopy of a page from the 1980 UCLA yearbook showing the CEO as a much younger man. He spoke perfect English, and Ryan knew it.

"Would you like a glass of wine?" she offers, while leading Ryan into the living room with its full wall sliding glass doors beckoning to the brick patio and swimming pool outside.

"Yes, please." Just the way Margaret stares at Ryan gives new meaning to the term *steel blue eyes*. There is no warmth at all. They penetrate into his very soul. He shivers.

How many pleasant evenings have been spent sitting around smelling the fragrances from the blossoming citrus trees or listening to the palm fronds rustling in the wind or the sounds from the nearby canal or just talking? Not about anything in particular, just talking.

Margaret approaches an antique side table and lifts a bottle of Polcino Chianti, filling the two glasses already placed on the tray. Ryan notices that the bottle has already been opened and there is a touch of red liquid in the bottom of one glass. He smiles to himself with the knowledge that she has had a nerve bracing starter.

Wait, Margaret had broken her own first rule: no red wine in the living room. This is completely understandable considering that the room is furnished completely in white, the only color coming from the several large contemporary paintings on the walls and from the bird of paradise plants standing watch. Paradise. Now, that in itself is ironic.

This is definitely not going to be a good evening. Tonight is the first time Ryan can remember when he has entered Margaret's house without music playing in the background. There were always sounds of classical, opera, or jazz music. It's another bad omen. Suddenly, it occurs to him that maybe he should leave. Just get up and go and whatever happens—happens. This whole mess is not his fault. But he can't leave, and he knows it. Ryan is sick to his stomach.

The interruption of telephone sounds like an explosion in contrast to the unsettling quiet in which they are sitting, simply staring at each other.

Margaret answers. "Hello. He just got here. I'll call you later. 'Bye."

"That was Ingrid."

"Do you think it absolutely necessary to bring someone else into this?" Ryan's voice is a little too edgy.

"I didn't tell her anything, except that you were coming over and we need to talk."

He shrugs.

"You know I don't have a choice," Margaret announces.

"You do have a choice. You have chosen to put your self-righteous nose into someone else's business," Ryan angrily responds.

"You're warped. How can you say that? Don't you realize how important this is?"

"To whom? You?"

"There are certain things that have to be done, and this is one of them."

"Maybe . . . but it's not yours to do."

"You're right. It's not mine to do. It's yours to do, but you won't."

"I can't, damn it, and you know it!"

"That's bullshit and *you* know it! Why'd you ever get me involved in the first place if you didn't want my opinion?" Her voice rises as she speaks.

"Because I love you . . . and I respect your opinion."

"Respect my opinion!" With snake-like speed, she uncoils from the couch and slides toward Ryan. "If you respect my opinion, why don't you pay attention to what I'm saying?"

"Just because I don't do what you want doesn't mean that I don't hear you!" Indignantly, Ryan springs to his feet to face Margaret. "Did it ever occur to you that you might possibly be wrong?"

"Wrong? You're blind and he has been your blind spot for as long as I've known you. Admit it! He's no good. Plain and simple. Any way you slice it, he's *no good*." The color rises in her cheeks as quickly as it drains from his.

"No! That's not quite accurate," she continues. Ryan relaxes for an instant. "He's simply a rotten lowlife scumbag who isn't worthy to clean toilets."

"You don't know what you're talking about!"

"Ryan, stop trying to defend him. He's a killer . . . a multiple killer . . . of innocent people . . . not just other creeps like himself, but whoever happens to be in his way. You've been trying to cover up for him since . . . like forever. Wake up, Ryan."

He stares at Margaret with a level of scorn he never thought possible. She has crossed the line and there is no turning back. The problem is exacerbated by the fact that she is right. Absolutely right! It has been a curse that Ryan has tried to exorcise since, well, for as long as he can remember. The conflict he feels is the worst pain he has ever experienced. He's trapped. *Back off, Margaret, it's my decision to make, not yours!* His head is pounding.

"Ryan . . . Ryan." Her voice penetrates the agony of the moment. "It's not an opinion. We're either going to go together or I'm going to go alone . . . tomorrow. End of discussion."

"End of discussion? I thought I came here to talk about things, not respond to an ultimatum." Ryan quickly closes to where Margaret is standing. Their eyes lock.

"It's not an ultimatum; it's a statement of fact. I'm going to do what's right. That's it." Her voice sends another chill throughout Ryan's body. He shivers.

"How can you abuse my trust like this? I told you everything in confidence. You have no right to breach that confidence." Ryan's anger is only exceeded by his sense of betrayal.

"You're rationalizing, Ryan. Making excuses for someone who doesn't deserve your blind loyalty. I can't let that happen . . . and I won't."

"For Christ's sake Margaret, get off your damn soap-box. This is absolutely none of your concern. Others can deal with it. It's not up to either of us." Ryan steps even closer to Margaret. Her body tenses.

"Of course it's our concern. It's very much our concern. It's everyone's concern. Why can't you see that?"

"You can't do this, Margaret. I won't permit it." Ryan's hands fall to his sides as he lowers his head.

Margaret begins to laugh . . . actually laugh. "What do you mean I can't, and you won't permit it? I don't need your permission."

Slowly, Ryan's entire body begins to visibly shake. All he can think of is stopping her laughter. He could strangle her. Margaret, the woman he loves. How can this be happening?

She reacts to some veiled danger she feels. Her eyes dart around the room to find the easiest way out. The doors to the patio are unlocked and close by. In two strides, she reaches the glass sliders and pulls on the handle. A blast of hot, stale air fills the room, drawing Ryan's attention from his self-absorption to Margaret's flight.

"What the hell do you think you're doing?" He demands.

"I'm getting out of here. You're crazy . . . obsessed."

"Obsessed? You're the one who wants to ruin everything," he replies.

"Everything? No way. We've got nothing."

Ryan crosses the room. Margaret steps over the threshold onto the patio—catching her heel on its metal track. She loses her balance. Ryan watches, in seemingly slow motion, as she pirouettes out of control onto the damp patio. Her head makes a sickening sound as it hits the hard brick surface.

"Margaret!" Ryan screams.

She lies motionless. He kneels next to her inert body. Margaret's vitality is forever gone.

"Jesus, Mary, and Joseph," he mutters.

The phone in the hall rings. He can't answer it. What could he possibly say? *Oh hi, Margaret and I had an argument and she fell, hit her head, and I think she's dead. Of course, it was an accident. It's not like I was threatening her or anything.*

Ryan's eyes return to Margaret's body. "They won't believe me, will they?" His head is pounding. He almost hears the mocking voice of a district attorney. *Now, Mr.*

McCallum, would you explain why Miss Adams felt it necessary to go outside on a damp night? To get a breath of fresh air? They wouldn't understand that Margaret would often sit out on her patio to think about things—rain or shine— warm or cool—day or night.

The telephone thankfully stops ringing. Maybe he should call the police and tell them the whole story. Well, at least part of the story. *What if they ask me what we were arguing about?* The voice of the faceless police investigator hammers in his head. Just go. Now. Just walk out the door, and if anyone asks you, say that when you left, she was fine. The telephone interrupts his thoughts.

Suddenly, an idea pops into his mind. It is simple. Move the body to the pool and push it in so that it looks like she was working in the flower bed, stood up, slipped, and fell, banged her head, and drowned. That way it will look like an accident. But that's what it is—an accident.

With almost superhuman strength, Ryan lifts Margaret's lifeless form and carries her across the brick patio to the edge of the pool. His luck momentarily returns when he spots a couple of flats of unplanted pansies and the trowel she had been using before he arrived. Perfect.

He can't believe this has really happened. It wasn't his fault. She should never have gotten involved.

He carefully rolls Margaret into the water. As an afterthought, he turns on the garden lights, retreats into the living room, closes the sliding door, and confronts another problem. There are two wineglasses from which they had been drinking. "Leave them," he says half-aloud. There is no way he's going to be able to get away from the fact that he was here tonight, so leave the glasses. She decided to go out after he left and putter in her precious garden. She's done it before. Only this time she slipped and fell. It's what happened . . . sort of.

Ryan takes one more look around the living room—slowly taking in all the details. The white walls, furniture and rug look sterile and somehow distant. He shakes his head. Why in God's name did this have to happen? What an unbelievable waste. What a tragedy. Preventable and unnecessary. A single tear forms at the corner of his eye as he walks down the path toward his car for the last time. He wraps his arms across his body as protection from the weather or maybe from himself. Shaking uncontrollably, he opens the Mercedes' door, quickly slides in, starts the engine, and backs down the driveway into the enveloping darkness.

CHAPTER TWO

Neighborhoods are fascinating sociological phenomena. Certainly this is true for folks who grew up in the '50s and '60s. On one hand, the neighborhood was a microcosm of a larger society—the one out there. While on the other hand, each neighborhood operated semi-autonomously from that same larger society.

Frequently, a neighborhood acquires certain groups of identifiers, either by virtue of location, the origin of its residents, or sometimes both. These identifiers brand those living within the increasingly vague and elastic boundaries: *He's a townie*; *She's from Southie*; or *They live in the flats*. Immediately one conjures up images and expectations, and in the process, labels someone from a specific neighborhood as having those certain characteristics. These assumptions are reflected upon all the residents generally—often very incorrectly. Being stigmatized thus, young men and women end up conforming to the mold in which their birthplace or happenstance of residency have thrust upon them, thereby giving the rather demeaning generalizations certain validity. Occasionally someone escapes and proves the exception to this very unfair rule.

One such neighborhood is Meadowdale Heights, whose elevated terrain allows residents the unique opportunity to examine, from a birds-eye view, the urban sprawl and decay in which they are also living and working. Maybe it makes them feel less motivated to escape, knowing that everyone is living pretty much the same as they are, unless, of course, you look toward the east. Then you see the towering, shining new buildings that form the heart of the city with the shimmering water beckoning to places far beyond. That's where those who are ultimately going to leave the Heights look for encouragement.

It's not that the Heights is a bad place to grow up. For the McCallum family it was, in many respects, ideal. Everything and everybody are within walking distance. In the age before latch-key kids, there were extended families; and here in Meadowdale most of the children who attend St. Mary's had grandparents, uncles, aunts, and cousins by the bushel living within the shadow cast by the great steeple. Of course, owning the local building supply store, where you could still buy nails from a barrel, makes the McCallum family a little better situated than many others. There is a passive aura of protectiveness in Meadowdale Heights, which gives the children a comfortable zone in which to play. Everyone is watching out for everyone else. It's different from being nosy. It's a real concern.

A further advantage, shared by most of the kids from the Heights, is that everyone, well almost everyone, attends St. Mary's. The schedule never changes: Monday through Friday, first grade through sixth at St. Mary's; Saturday, youth basketball or baseball, depending on the season, at St. Mary's; Saturday evenings, dances at St. Mary's; Sunday morning, cataclysm classes at St. Mary's. And then you start all over again. It isn't bad. It is simply the same—year in, year out—forever, or so it seems.

It is the same for Ryan and Sean McCallum, identical twin sons of Patrick and Maria McCallum, grandsons of Sean and Patricia McCallum and Ryan and Victoria O'Neil.

Technically, twins are two children born about the same time from the same mother. Twins are more common than you'd think—about once in every ninety births. Twins can be either fraternal or identical. The former develops when two separate eggs are fertilized at about the same time. Anyway, identical twins are produced as the result of a single fertilized egg splitting in two. Each half develops as a separate fetus, but with identical genes. There are several additional twin anomalies: including so-called mirror image twins, who are identical, but in reverse.

Ryan was the Yang to Sean's Ying. Even though they were identical, they were opposite. Ryan is right-handed while Sean was left-handed. Ryan is an excellent student—not so with Sean. They are, however, inextricably bound together by genetic forces which merely augment the way in which their surroundings deal with them. There is nothing one wouldn't do for the other.

No one remembers when they first noticed the difference—that basic, most fundamental difference between the twins. Maybe it was when their father brought home a brand-new kitten that had been given to him by a customer at the store. He was a calico with bright green eyes. The brothers were almost five, and both Patrick and Maria thought that by giving them a pet, they would be helping Sean and Ryan develop a sense of responsibility—feeding and playing with the kitty, and of course cleaning the litter box. While Ryan demonstrated both skill and enthusiasm, Sean saw the cat, who they had named Butch, as an imposition. His attitude went beyond indifference. He was mean, actually cruel, to the poor creature who wanted nothing more from him than to be loved.

One time, just to see what would happen next, Sean poured some vinegar into Butch's water dish. Fortunately, even at two months old, a kitten is empowered with primal instinct, and he refused to drink. It was only after several hours of constant meowing that Maria McCallum finally picked up the bowl and smelled the bitter liquid. She never said anything to either Sean or Ryan, and certainly never breathed a word to Mr. McCallum, although she undoubtedly held a suspicion of exactly what had happened.

This incident is far from being isolated within the McCallum household. Early on, loose change would disappear from Maria's purse or coat pocket. While she would attribute the lost money to memory lapses, deep inside, she knew, and it broke her heart. Sean's behavior, coupled with the fact that the McCallum's were not able to have any additional children after the birth of the twins, caused Maria to begin disengaging from the men in her family. Slowly at first.

After the boys were enrolled in a preschool program at St. Mary's, when they were about five and a half, Maria became increasingly reclusive. On a nice warm morning, she might be found walking along the tree-lined sidewalk along Santa Teresa Boulevard, going nowhere in particular. Regardless, duty always prevails, and at noon each day she would pick up the children, but only after she makes a quick visit to recite morning prayers at St. Mary's magnificent neo-Gothic chapel. Maria always enjoys these truly spiritual moments. It is so much more fulfilling than Mass on Sunday, which seems strangely like a command performance—an encore, rather than an outreach to the Lord. Maria loves her private, quiet times.

Sadly, her husband, Patrick hardly notices. He is a creature of habit—he rises early, usually by five o'clock. His ritual never changes. He makes himself a cup of strong Columbian coffee, which he grinds fresh daily. Someone once said that he got the grinder as a sample to be used in demonstrations in the store and got hooked on fresh coffee beans. The aroma of the brew wafts throughout the McCallum house. Well, actually, half the house, since the McCallum's live in a two-family structure, indistinguishable from any other two-family in the Heights.

After he reverently pours the first cup of coffee, still wearing his robe and slippers, Patrick McCallum retrieves the morning paper from the front porch. After reading the paper, cover to cover, he showers, shaves, and dresses in gray slacks; a white shirt, and plain, solid color and a too narrow to be fashionable tie—seven days a week.

Monday through Saturday, he leaves the house by six fifteen and begins his walk to the store, which he opens promptly at 7 a.m. *The early bird catches the worm* is his favorite expression, and Mr. McCallum believes that by opening an hour earlier than any of the box stores, he will get more contractor business, which might make the difference between success and failure to a small hardware store owner, even if you have to offer substantial *builder discounts*.

On Sunday, dressed as always, Patrick McCallum walks to St. Mary's to attend early Mass, returns home, wakes the boys so they can get ready for catechism class, cooks bacon and eggs—always exactly the same way, and returns to St. Mary's with Sean and Ryan. The only variance in his schedule is if the weather is so horrible, usually defined as a hurricane or a nor'easter, and he is forced to drive Ryan and Sean. After leaving the boys, he meets with a number of other men from the neighborhood. Whatever they say or do is never repeated at home. And so, his Sundays, after church, remain a mystery.

Maria attends Sunday Mass at 9:30, mostly to keep up appearances. She then retrieves the boys from their class, which by then has been reduced to chaos, despite the best efforts of whichever young priest has the bad luck to be designated as teacher of the faith to the youngsters of the Heights. Usually, on the way home, Maria stops and picks up a few things, while the boys beg, plead, or otherwise impose their will upon her to buy them a treat. After returning home, the twins keep to themselves, usually occupied by watching TV, until they become old enough to hang out with their friends, many of whom are older and decidedly less savory than Maria McCallum would like. But what could she do?

Maria's routine is as well-established as that of her husband, especially on Sunday. Upon return from church, she changes out of her *Sunday* clothes, dons a simple house-dress, and sets herself up in the kitchen to prepare a full Sunday dinner to be served promptly at four—no exceptions, not even for the World Series or an earthquake. The guest list is the only thing that ever varies. With so many members of both Patrick's and Maria's families living within a stone's throw, and because of Maria's reputation as a fabulous cook, an invitation to the McCallum home for a Sunday dinner is coveted, except, of course, that the boys hate it.

The proverbial straw that breaks the camel's back, in this case Maria's, came at a Sunday dinner when the boys had just turned twelve. Not surprisingly. It might be what led up to the day which set the stage for what was to follow.

As a child, even as a young man, it never had occurred to Ryan to talk back to his parents, to the nuns at St. Mary's, or actually to anyone older than he was or anyone in authority. But Sean, the opposite, *had a mouth on him*, so reported his teachers. Maybe it was a matter of personal initiative or maybe it was innate curiosity or maybe there was simply something *wrong* with Sean. From the moment the McCallum twins entered school, the results could have been predicted; Ryan would always be among the top of his class, while Sean would barely get by. Ryan took pride in his work, which was always completed on time. Sean's homework is always thrown together and often late and never reflective of diligence or care.

In the classroom, Sean is frequently reprimanded for fooling around, which at St. Mary's usually means a rap on the knuckles with a ruler, while Ryan is constantly praised for his participation and seriousness. And then there were the headaches—blinding headaches that are so severe tears would form in Sean's eyes. At first everyone assumed that Sean simply needed glasses, but his vision tested perfectly, better than 20/20.

Maria frequently notices Sean rubbing the side of his head, but whenever she asks him, *what's wrong, dear?* He smugly answers with some flip remark, like *I'm massaging my brain so I can be as smart as Ryan.* Then he'll laugh and walk away. Maria sighs deeply and resumes whatever she is doing.

By the time the boys are in second grade, it becomes increasingly apparent that while Ryan loves to read for personal pleasure, Sean will do anything, even help with the chores, to avoid picking up a book. After the twins go to bed at night, Sean can be heard asking Ryan to tell him about what he is reading. Sean has the uncanny ability to process information once told to him, and Sean McCallum never, ever, forgot anything or anyone.

It was in the context of all this that the McCallum's sat down for Sunday dinner on that rainy and cold March day. The first Sunday following the beginning of Lent.

CHAPTER THREE

One thing that never ceases to be a source of amazement is how a dozen people can witness the same event—an automobile accident, for example, and no two will recall the details in even a remotely similar fashion. I suppose it is analogous to the parlor game where one person tells another some fact or incident, and they in turn tell another and so on. Well, by the time everyone has heard and repeated the story, it bears no resemblance to the original. This is how *Sean's tale*, as it is now called, was passed throughout the McCallum family and beyond.

It should have been a Sunday dinner, not unlike any other Sunday dinner. Uncle Eli and Aunt Margaret have been invited to partake, along with their children: Kenneth, a tall, thin, red-headed seventeen-year-old with a nose like a hawk, bad complexion, and a high-pitched voice, and Linda, a slightly overweight just turned fifteen-year-old, with the long blonde stringy hair then in fashion. Linda has the annoying habit of pursing her lips after every sentence she speaks.

Mrs. McCallum holds the belief that eight is the perfect number of people to have at a dinner table. Enough to serve a proper roast with several side dishes, but not too many to prevent a single conversation, usually dominated by Patrick McCallum. As head of the household, Mr. McCallum enjoys his prerogative to *share* his political opinions with everyone and anyone. Dissent is not encouraged.

There must have been warning signs, but no one admits having seen them; or if they did, they chose to ignore them. In retrospect, three adolescent boys and one shy and sensitive teenage girl at a table together, for what must seem like forever, on a raw, damp, and dreary March afternoon, without the opportunity to go outside and blow off some steam shooting hoops or playing street hockey, is a formula for disaster. Only it struck in a way that would have been hard to predict.

"Eli, if I've said it once, I've said it a thousand times, the government has no policy for the Middle East. None whatsoever," Mr. McCallum addresses his brother-in-law, and presumably everyone else at the table. "Our boys are getting their asses shot off and for what?"

"Patrick!" Maria shouts. "Your language. There are young, impressionable children at the table." That may have been part of the problem—just how out of touch Maria McCallum is with the world at large, and especially her children.

"And we've never heard about asses, Mom," Sean flatly asserts. "Like we've been sitting on ours all day." Ryan stars at his brother, then immediately shifts his gaze to his father, who seems to have suspended his monologue in mid-word.

"Young man, please excuse yourself from the table, this instant," Mrs. McCallum demands, showing extraordinary restraint under the circumstances.

"What for?" Sean belligerently replies. "What's the big deal? Everyone knows what the word means. At St. Mary's, they even say Linda is a piece of it." An evil smirk settles across Sean's face, but only for an instant.

Ken's open right hand smacks Sean across his cheek. "Don't you talk about my sister that way!"

In less than the blink of an eye, Sean grabs a fork from the table and stabs his cousin in the hand with almost superhuman strength, burying the tines in the exposed flesh, practically pinning his hand to the table.

"Don't ever touch me again . . . faggot."

The scene that follows is worthy of Alfred Hitchcock's best. For an instant, no one moves or speaks. Nothing happens at all, except that blood begins to spread over Maria's snow-white tablecloth. It is like a frame of a motion picture frozen upon the screen. Then all hell breaks loose. The furies are released. The four horsemen ride upon the world, well, at least the world of the McCallum family.

I'm not sure if anyone thought about the consequences of what is to follow. More likely than not, it really didn't make any difference. It is inevitable.

The patriarch of the McCallum family remains in his chair at the head of the table, unmoving, while both sisters, Maria and Margaret, spring into action, albeit in opposite ways.

The younger and more impacted sibling, Margaret, immediately rushes to the side of her now-screaming children; Linda, who is simply being hysterical for the sake of hysteria, and Kenneth, from his obvious pain. After yanking the fork—cum—weapon from his bloody hand, Margaret wraps the wounded fist in a white linen napkin, which had been in her lap only seconds before. She orders Kenneth to elevate his hand.

"Keep it above your heart. Eli . . ." she continues. "Get up and call the police!"

"The police?" Patrick McCallum yells, awakening from his stupor. "We don't need the police. It's a family matter."

"It has nothing to do with family! My son is bleeding, and he needs emergency medical care for Christ's sake!" Margaret shrieks, shocking her pious sister. Maria reacts predictably. She crosses herself.

"I think the rescue squad is with the fire department," Ryan calmly inserts into the disintegrating scene. "I'll call." He rises and moves through the chaos to the relative peace and quiet of the living room, and the telephone.

As Linda is about to impart something most likely useless, her mother stares at her with burning eyes and warns, "Not a word, young lady. Not a single word." Linda sobbingly gasps.

In contrast to the relative efficiency of her younger sister, Maria rushes into the kitchen and returns to the crisis with a damp kitchen towel, which she places on the blood-stain left on the tablecloth by the assault upon Kenneth's hand. She gently blots the red mark in the same manner as if some guest had inadvertently spilled some red wine.

Only Sean remains, at least on the surface, completely unaffected by the goings-on. His gaze roams from one person to the next. A sadistic kind of smile returns to his lips. Although the protagonist in this drama, Sean is now relegated to the role of a spectator. After a few minutes, unaccustomed to being outside the center of attention and impatient with passivity, especially being in the midst of the craziness of what had been the McCallum family dinner, Sean slowly rises from his seat, "I think I'll skip dessert tonight."

Stunned into silence, everyone at the table freezes. Ryan stands alone at the door to the living room, absorbing the scene before him.

Mr. McCallum is heard over the shouts of the others. "Just who the fuck do you think you are?"

Sean, in yet another defiant moment, simply shrugs.

"I should beat you within an inch of your life!" His father warns.

"So?" Sean replies. "Like you really give a shit."

Maria McCallum gasps, crosses herself again and screams. "Don't you dare talk to your father that way! It's, it's . . . disrespectful!"

Sean's grin widens. His father might very well have struck him with every ounce of his being at that instant, except that the wailing of a siren announces the arrival of medical assistance for the simpering Kenneth and his mangled mitt.

CHAPTER FOUR

Consistency and stability are frequently viewed as synonymous. Not so in the McCallum family. Day in, day out, the routine remains the same, but the fragility of the family unit is evident looking from the inside out. Looking from the outside in, everything seems normal—more or less. That probably explains why both Ryan and Sean feel the need to escape. Only they escape differently. Ryan dedicates himself to academics, athletics, and the community and so does Sean, although in quite the opposite way.

Ryan is in every way the *perfect child*. He is accepted at the prestigious Boston Latin School and spends his high school years doing everything right. He participates in every aspect of school life. He not only participates . . . he excels. Whether as a member of the football or baseball teams, both of which he captains as a senior, or as a member of the National Honor Society, Ryan is liked by peers and teachers alike.

Unfortunately, neither of his parents appreciate nor understand his success. Maybe *not appreciate* is too harsh. They simply never embrace his efforts. Other than graduation, where he wins the coveted Harvard Book prize, neither McCallum parent ever attends a school event. That probably serves as a motivator for Ryan to do even better. He even joins the St. Mary's choir, whether because he likes singing or because he knows that at least his mother will notice, even if he doesn't fully understand.

Sean never lacks attention, albeit from police and juvenile authorities. Sean routinely skips school and does errands for some local *wise guys*. By the time he reaches his sixteenth birthday, Sean has been arrested four times for minor crimes—assuming breaking and entering and grand theft auto are minor. Sean always has a pocket full of money and certain people to help him out of jams.

Despite these differences there is an incredible bond between the twins. In contrast to his parents, Sean never misses a game in which his brother plays. Ryan is inwardly pleased, but sometimes needs to distance himself from Sean because of his reputation. This doesn't bother Sean. He understands. He never feels slighted. He actually feels proud that his *bad guy* reputation precedes him. Sean is also very generous to his brother. Once when Ryan needed a new blazer for school but had deferred getting it because he certainly didn't want to ask his father and hadn't earned enough from the odd jobs he fits in around his hectic schedule, Sean takes the subway into Cambridge, walks over to Brooks Brothers and purchases, with cash, a new blue blazer with brass buttons for Ryan. He even buys him a new regimental striped tie to go with the new threads. Obviously, if it fits Sean, it will fit his brother.

Ryan is speechless. This is the other side of Sean. The side that makes Ryan always come to his brother's defense—no matter what.

For as long as Sean is a minor, the Court system does little to encourage him to modify his behavior, which only gets worse. By the time Sean turns 18, he has only earned two years of high school credits. Needless to say, he drops out on his birthday. The strange thing is that Sean's transcript is dotted with honors grades in subjects that are verbal based. He earned an A+ in Western Philosophy. He also earns the right to leave the McCallum household, which he does without even saying good-bye.

It also means that Sean is going to have to get a job. It is a logical transition from being an errand boy to something more. Sean gets a promotion. And the money is good.

Ryan's path is also logical. His academic credentials earned him acceptance at Harvard, on scholarship. Maria McCallum pleads with Ryan to commute to school, but is overruled, to Ryan's great relief, by his father who says *Harvard wants to educate him, feed him, and give him a room on their nickel, why should we spend money?* Patrick McCallum's logic is irrefutable. If Ryan had been able to predict what would happen next, he might have re-thought his decision. But foresight is not a concept an eighteen-year-old boy possesses. Actually, most people lack foresight.

Ryan needs to get a summer job so that he can have some spending money during the academic year. He most definitely tries to avoid the inevitable working for his father. Sean makes some suggestions, which Ryan quickly rejects. No surprise. Just when all seems hopeless, Ryan's high school English teacher calls. Apparently, he had just been awarded a grant to write a book on literature in the American Colonies before the Revolution and the stipend was large enough to hire a research assistant. Since Harvard and the Boston Public library together, between them, have

the finest collection of 17th and 18th century literary manu-
scripts in the country, Ryan's summer is spent in academic
bliss. He also is able to get a *leg up* on most incoming
freshman. Ryan's casual and friendly demeanor make it
easy for him to meet students and members of the faculty.
He becomes familiar with the maze of Harvard buildings,
as well as the most popular hangouts.

Sometimes, Sean meets his brother after *work,* and they
grab a bite to eat and talk. Sean is truly interested in Ryan's
research, and he is more than willing to tell Sean about the
incredible literary talent that lived in Colonial America.
Ryan really does not want to hear about Sean's activities.

With Sean out of the house and Ryan soon to follow,
Maria's daily routine breaks down. She sometimes walks
aimlessly for hours. Nevertheless, she is never unkempt. She
does not have that bag lady look, but Maria is simply lost
and alone.

It probably comes as no surprise that Maria is found
dead in her bed only three weeks after Ryan starts his
freshman year. There is speculation and gossip that Maria
committed suicide, but most who knew her accept that she
died of a broken heart.

CHAPTER FIVE

Believe it or not, the loss of their mother did not affect Ryan as much as it did Sean. Although Ryan has always been seen as the more sensitive brother, Sean's connection to his mother is obviously very strong. Sean slowly withdraws from his friends and finally his brother— not returning Ryan's calls. People begin to comment that they haven't seen Sean hanging around anymore. Ryan really doesn't give it a lot of thought since he is totally consumed by the college experience. And Sean can take care of himself. Maybe Ryan should be more assertive and reach out to his brother, but both the academic and social demands at Harvard are a full-time job. Also, Ryan has virtually no connections with the old neighborhood. Other than a weekly Sunday brunch with his roommate, Stephen Blackman, Ryan's absorption into academia is complete.

Patrick McCallum's routine changes little from all outward appearances. The patriarch of the family does not keep in touch with either of his sons. Maybe he thinks they are best on their own or maybe he simply doesn't think about it at all. When everything falls apart, doing the same thing you've always done is somehow comforting. At least it allows you to get from day to day. But to what end? That's a different issue.

As the Christmas break looms ahead, Ryan briefly thinks about home and all the things that will never be the same; his mom's smile, the family dinners, the arguments, and visiting relatives whom he only sees once a year despite the fact that they live within a few miles. It becomes an easy choice. He elects to stay in his dorm and prepare for exams which Harvard holds after Christmas, rather than before like every other college.

Ryan calls his brother's phone several times during the holidays. The number is disconnected. His father says he hasn't heard from *that no-good kid* in months, and *he doesn't care*. Other than attending midnight mass, Ryan continues his push back from his roots.

New Year's Eve comes and goes. Students return to renew the routine of preparing for and taking exams. And then two weeks off. Ryan is saved from deciding what to do when his roommate suggests that the two of them go skiing in Vermont. Well, not exactly *go skiing*, since Ryan has never even been to a ski slope—money and time being a major factor, and Stephen, who grew up in central Florida, has only skied on water and usually with temperatures around 80-degrees.

They pack, pool their money, and walk to the subway station. The Red Line takes them to South Station. They wait to board a bus to Burlington, Vermont. Suddenly, out of the corner of his eye Ryan catches a glimpse of Sean. At least he thinks it's Sean. The person is moving fast. He is in

the company of two other men—large and mean-looking.
The threesome stop, look around, and continue their
journey. As it turns out, that is the last time Ryan sees his
brother for over ten years. Needless to say, the paths of the
brothers McCallum will cross again.

Ryan's undergraduate years pass with alarming speed.
Suddenly, he is attending, alone, his own graduation,
magna cum laude, from Harvard College with an acceptance in hand to Harvard Business School. His roommate
and best friend, who also graduates with honors, has his
own acceptance letter—to Harvard Law School. Needless
to say, they decide to room together in a small apartment in
Antrim Square about two miles from Harvard Yard.

Graduate school is even more demanding than undergraduate studies. Ryan elects to spend three years at the
Business School, rather than the normal two years so that
he can participate in several intern programs that give him
real-life business experience as well as money to complete
his course of study. Since Stephen's course of study at the
Law School requires three years, the two best friends enter
the real world at the same time.

Ryan thinks that employment within the financial
community will be exciting, challenging, and very lucrative. Upon graduation, he receives an offer to work at
Simpson, Tucker & Co., a boutique financial advisory firm.
Basically, they manage other people's money, but only very
wealthy other people. Not only does the job bring with
it the opportunity to earn a six-digit income, including
a performance bonus, but also allows Ryan to sever the
last of his old ties. Simpson, Tucker, and Co. is located

in Orlando, which is experiencing incredible growth. Ironically, Stephen Blackman is offered a clerkship to an associate justice of the Massachusetts Supreme Court. The roommates have effectively switched "hometowns".

CHAPTER SIX

Suffice it to say that relocating to Florida is for Ryan, *just what the doctor ordered*. His employers immediately recognize his work ethic, inherent brilliance, and wonderful *bedside manner*, which immediately draws new clients to him like the proverbial moth to a flame.

Within five years, Ryan has earned a partnership and his six-digit salary is now bordering on seven digits. Despite the distance and his incredible success, he and Stephen remain very close. Every year they plan a couple of one-week vacations together. Although they talk about going to Europe, where neither has visited, the demands of their respective careers limit their vacations to exploring the environs of either New England or Florida. Ryan excludes the old neighborhood from his itinerary, while Stephen always hooks up with old friends and family whenever he returns to Florida.

As they each climb the ladder, it is not surprising that after partnership; Ryan at Simpson, Tucker, and Stephen at Smith, Wilcott, and Franklin, a very old, prestigious Boston law firm, marriage will follow.

The next year finds Ryan proposing to Judith Lynne Rosemont of the Birmingham, Alabama Rosemont's, and Stephen requesting the hand of Ruth Chapman in marriage. There is no question that each young lady will accept. Ryan and Stephen are seriously good catches with nothing but a great and comfortable future ahead. Crystal balls have a way of being misread.

While Ryan is climbing the corporate ladder his twin brother is steadily climbing his own corporate ladder—sort of. Actually, Sean is "made" partner about the same time as Ryan, although each with slightly different employers. As much as Ryan impresses the folks at Simpson, Tucker, with his work ethic, inherent brilliance, and wonderful *bedside manner*; Sean impresses his employer with his work ethic, inherent ruthlessness, and wonderful *graveside manner*.

From being an errand boy to being a "made wise guy" for an Irish kid from the Heights, is unheard of, but Sean McCallum is really good at his job. Ryan is only tangentially aware of his brother's unsavory occupation. Actually, he chooses to ignore it as much as possible.

It has been almost a decade since their paths crossed last. Maybe it's Ryan's engagement announcement in the newspaper that gets Sean thinking about his twin. Maybe it's his father's death. Maybe it's a coincidence, but Sean doesn't believe in coincidences.

There is more than a little irony that both the McCallum twins end up in the financial services industry albeit at opposite ends of the spectrum. Although they look exactly the same, one is Ying and the other Yang.

Sean's overture to Ryan comes in the form of an envelope hand delivered to his office. The receptionist at

Simpson, Tucker knocks on Ryan's door, which he always keeps slightly open.

"Come in Liz. What can I do for you?"

"Mr. McCallum, this envelope just came by a messenger who was very insistent that I hand it to you . . . immediately."

"Thank you." Ryan rises from his green leather chair and reaches across the desk. He looks at the writing on the envelope. "Liz, what did the messenger who delivered this letter look like?"

"He was young. No more than twenty with red hair and emerald, green eyes. He looked like an ad for Aer Lingus. He was really cute." A slight blush brightens Liz's cheeks.

"Thanks again," Ryan says. He waits until Liz leaves. "Oh Liz, please close the door." Ryan quickly opens the envelope.

The contents consist of a typed letter and a cashier's check in the amount of $8,000.

Ryan,

I know it's been a while, but it has taken me longer than I expected to get my shit together. I am no longer associated with the Dagos but have opened my own business which has been very successful.

I am thinking more responsibly than ever before. I think I should start a brokerage account and who is more qualified and trustworthy to oversee my money than you? I want to sock money away for the rainy day I hope never happens. The investments should be conservative and growth oriented.

I will be wiring money into my account weekly. Never more than $10,000 at a time. I want you to be the beneficiary if something happens to me. I also want to designate St. Mary's as the backup beneficiary.

Can you imagine the look on the sisters' if they see a donation from Sean McCallum? What a hoot.

By the way, we are almost neighbors. I have moved to Miami.

To open my account you will need my social security number which is the same as yours expect the last digit is a 7. My address is P.O. Box 3519, Miami Beach, FL. 33141. Hopefully, we can get in touch with one another for something other than business.

Love,
Sean

Ryan's heart beats at twice the normal rate. He reads the note again. It is vintage Sean—always holding the cards close to his vest. Like making it clear that the amounts of money he will be depositing will always be under the $10,000 reporting requirement and not putting his social security in writing, but rather relying on Ryan to put it on the necessary forms. He also does not want his brother to know where he actually lives, using a post office box instead. However, nothing is illegal.

Ryan is torn. One side of him demands *"return the money and have nothing more to do with him"* while the other side counsels, *"he's your brother, your twin brother and you should do whatever you can to help him."* The latter wins and Ryan opens the account, deposits the money into the account and sends the paperwork to Sean to sign and return. Ryan wonders whether he will rue the day he decides that blood was thicker than—anything else.

Like clockwork, every week Sean sends a wire to Ryan to invest in his account. The amounts vary from $5,000 to $9,000 but, as promised, never exceed $10,000. Sean's account grows by a combination of new additions and Ryan's expertise. By year's end, Sean's account is valued at over a half million dollars. Not bad for a high school dropout.

Ryan applies his investment acumen to his other clients, as well. He becomes the top performer at Simpson, Tucker, exceeding all the senior partners, which at first makes everyone smile, but later creates a lot of tension.

Wedding plans also consume much of Ryan's time; although he tends to let Judith, who moves into Ryan's condominium in Orlando, handle everything. First of all, Ryan isn't interested in the details of the wedding. He would prefer a small, intimate affair on a beach somewhere, but the Rosemont's of Birmingham only want the best for their darling daughter, and only child. The fact that Judith spends so much time with her mother doing whatever mothers and daughters do to prepare for a wedding, gives Ryan extra time at the office.

Since sitting down with Judith at dinner is not required on a regular basis, Ryan starts a regimen of riding his bike after work—sometimes for hours. The lengthening spring days allow him to ride until 9:00 o'clock in sunlight. He enjoys feeling invigorated and is in great shape. Actually, when Judith returns from her visits to Birmingham, Ryan's life seems confined, limited in some way. He dismisses these responses to pre-nuptial jitters. Heck, he has until

Labor Day to work through any reservations. He is assigned the task of putting together a guest list "*from the groom's side.*"

CHAPTER SEVEN

Trying to come up with whom he wants to invite to his wedding is a far more difficult task than Ryan has ever imagined. It's not actually coming up with names, but it is a matter of confronting his past. Other than Sean, who is always questionable, he has not maintained a relationship with anyone from the Heights. Most of the older generation have died or are too far gone to either travel or remember who Ryan is, and those cousins who are more or less contemporaries have long ago vanished from his radar screen. Back to Sean. Why not? Ryan convinces himself that Sean will not embarrass himself or more importantly Judith and her rather inflexible and overbearing family. Sean can simply be introduced as his twin brother—a South Florida businessman.

Ryan considers arranging a lunch or dinner between Judith and Sean so that they can at least recognize one another at the wedding. Other than Stephen Blackman, there is no one from his college and graduate school days Ryan wants to add to the *groom's list*. Judith will most likely include at least a zillion of all her old *friends*.

There are a couple of people from the office he should invite, although they are not what he considers social acquaintances. Ryan wonders if he has trouble making friends. Is he too fussy? He has never really given it much thought. It's quality not quantity. Right?

Thank the Lord, that's settled. He is going to invite Sean and a date, if he wants to bring one, and Stephen and Susan. From the office, Charles Simpson, III, grandson of the founder, who became a partner along with Ryan, and his wife, Virginia, about whom Ryan can't even muster the energy to dislike, even though she is a terrible snob and very boring. Frank Nichols is about ten years older than Ryan and a truly nice guy who mentored him through the Simpson, Wolcott mine field, should be added to the list. Notwithstanding the fact that Birmingham society feathers might be ruffled, Ryan is going to invite Robert Locke, Frank's partner, in the emotional sense. Frank and Robert have been together almost twenty years and when Florida finally permitted same sex marriages, they were first in line to get their license. That's seven for Ryan and about one hundred and fifty for Judith.

When he gives his list to his betrothed, she just stars at the paper and shakes her head. Disgust—anger—bewilderment? Ryan can't tell and quite frankly, does not give a damn.

"Is that all, honey?" She purrs.

"Should I add more?" Ryan replies.

"Only if you want to, dear," Judith says.

"No, I'm good."

Why does he feel so terrible? So guilty? He didn't do anything wrong. The harbinger of things to come.

The wedding plans keep Judith very busy. But what will keep her busy after they marry? A family? A house to manage? Social events to plan and attend? Ryan is not sure he is really ready for all this. A sense of uneasiness starts to encroach into his everyday life. He feels the walls closing in—his breathing is constricted. He writes it off as jitters and makes it a point not to change his bike riding routine. It brings him peace.

About three weeks before the wedding, Judith again returns to Birmingham to get ready for the blessed event. She never asks Ryan about his religious affiliation or for that matter about anything to do with the wedding—music, food, decorations, or the person who is going to perform the ceremony, who turns out to be a self-righteous, holier than thou bigot, which includes Catholics.

After Judith, once again, has left for "home" in Birmingham, Ryan grabs the first plane to Boston so that he can sit down with Stephen and confess his now mounting reservations about the wedding and into the future. One of his biggest concerns is Judith's obsessive connection with her family, especially her mother. Ryan fearfully imagines Judith insisting that they visit Birmingham at least twice a month and inviting her family to Orlando for holidays and other special occasions—the definition of which is somewhat up in the air. Ryan had been perfectly happy before Judith inserted herself into his life. Why is he set on screwing up everything? He doesn't need to get married. His employment opportunities are not going to increase. He hasn't given the possibility of children a lot of thought. What the hell is he doing?

Always the lawyer, Stephen asks Ryan whether he has thought about a pre-nuptial agreement. Of course not.

Stephen suggests that maybe he should talk to Judith's father who may want to insulate the Rosemont family assets from the newest member of the family—Ryan McCallum of Boston.

"Look old buddy," Stephen says, "I really want you to have the agreement so that if things don't work out, you will be whole. If it comes from old man Rosemont, it will be his idea, not yours. I can't offer you any advice about how to feel, but I can offer advice on how not to have money become the controlling factor in any decision you make."

"Are you and Susan happy?"

"I think so. There is a whole bunch of change that goes along with marriage. Compromises that I never thought about . . . and more on the way."

"What do you mean *more on the way*?" Ryan asks.

"Susan is pregnant."

"That's awesome. Big changes are on the way. Are you excited?"

"Yeah, I guess so. It really hasn't sunk in yet, but I think that everything is going to be good."

"That's comforting. I think you guys will be fine. I feel somewhat overwhelmed by the whole wedding process." Ryan is clearly torn.

"Do you want me to talk to Mr. Rosemont about a pre-nuptial agreement, subtly of course," Stephen asks.

"Are you sure it's a good idea?"

"Absolutely! Now, you can concentrate on important things, like making sure you put the toilet seat down." They both start to laugh hysterically.

And so ends the pre-wedding jitters.

CHAPTER EIGHT

The wedding goes as expected—totally overdone, overwhelming, over the top. Ryan simply smiles and nods to the well-wishers, which did not include Sean who had sent a note that he would be unable to attend. No explanation is given. The note had no return address but is postmarked *West Palm Beach*. Ryan is somewhat hurt by his brother's absence, but is neither angry nor surprised. What does surprise him is the regular stream of money from Sean—every week, like clockwork.

His marriage is neither great nor bad. As expected, the Rosemont's visit regularly—well actually Judith's mother. The two disappear for hours and sometimes days to shop. Fortunately, Mrs. Rosemont does most of the purchasing, so when her stay ends, her Jaguar is chock-a-block full of *stuff*. Ryan's father-in-law occasionally issues an invitation to go hunting or play in a golf tournament. Ryan always finds some kind of conflict—initially work related and then Margaret related. Judith would then scamper off to Birmingham to show family loyalty and make the necessary apologies.

The inevitable happens after almost eight years of
this charade, but not the way one would have expected.
Judith, her mother and Judith's sorority sister, Kimberly, are
planning to shop on Worth Avenue in Palm Beach, about
a three-hour drive from Orlando. Ryan decides to spend
the sun-drenched day playing golf. He enjoys walking the
course, which is a good thing because his game is terrible.
When he returns home, his first reaction is that his house
had been robbed in his absence, but then he realizes that
only Judith's things are gone, plus a few pieces of furniture from her family. A *Dear Ryan* letter is taped to the
refrigerator.

> I simply couldn't bear to confront you. By the
> time you read this, I'll be on my way home with mom
> and Kim. I only took my stuff. Daddy insisted upon
> that since it is really my fault.
>
> I guess I never got over Ronny, even after
> we were married. Remember he was my beaux
> at college. I saw him a lot when I went back to
> Birmingham. Last month I decided I wanted to
> spend the rest of my life with him. I will agree to
> the divorce and sign anything you want. I just need
> to be with him.
>
> I feel like a creep hurting you, but it is
> what it is.

A curious smile creeps across Ryan's face. Maybe he
should play golf more often. He has been worrying about
how to tell Judith about Margaret, but she beat him to
the punch. He picks up his cell phone and dials Stephen's
number.

"Guess what?"

"You broke 80."

"Even better."

"There is no way you completed an entire round better than that unless you were playing miniature golf."

"Even better."

"Cut the crap. What are you talking about?"

"Judith left. She took her things and confessed she was having a relationship with her old boyfriend. She's gone. Lock, stock, and barrel."

"No shit!"

"I'm going to scan the letter and send it to you. I want you to handle the legal side of things."

"I'm not admitted to the bar in Florida."

"Get a friend to handle going to court. I want you to do the paperwork. Bullet proof, Stephen, absolutely friggin' bullet proof."

"Done. If I have any questions, I will send you an email. Until everything is signed, sealed, and delivered, keep a lid on things. I suggest you handle Margaret carefully . . . also Judith. *Hell hath no fury.*"

"Thanks, old buddy. I ducked the bullet this time. I promise not to push my luck."

"Ryan . . . be well, safe, and happy." Stephen hangs up.

Was it a feeling of relief or one of remorse? Why feel remorse? Ryan did everything he could have been expected to do. Well almost everything. What's the old expression? *When a window closes, a door opens.* Something like that. Stephen is right. Better be cool until the divorce is done. Judith's father and he always got along. Her dad is not the, *what did you do to my little girl type.* Ryan hopes her new/old friend can afford to keep her in the style to which she has become accustomed and believes she richly deserves. At least her mother and she can shop closer to home. Suddenly, it occurs to Ryan that he should have asked Stephen about his bank accounts, retirement accounts, stock accounts and whatever. Should he try to keep his income down? Shit. Maybe he really needs to fly up to Boston and sit with him. The familiar sound of an incoming message on his cell phone wakens him from these dark deep thoughts. He looks at the screen. It's an email from Stephen.

It reads: "Here are your immediate marching orders: make sure all checking, stock, money market or saving accounts are in your sole name unless they are accounts that have had contributions from both of you. Change the beneficiary of your retirement accounts to 'The estate of Ryan McCallum.' Likewise change your P.O.D. to your estate. I will prepare a will for you. Please think about who you want to be a beneficiary. Maybe Sean? You can deal with Margaret at some later time. Don't go out and buy a new Tesla, and do not manipulate your income. I will call you tomorrow. Stephen"

That didn't take long. He is a great lawyer and a good friend. Ryan now has to figure out what to say to Margaret. Should he tell her about Judith's departure? She'll figure out that something is not quite right. Let's hope that Judith is desperate to get this over with. Maybe she's pregnant. Now wouldn't that be a twist. Not so fast. If she has a child while still technically married, even if it's her boyfriend's, Ryan could be on the hook for child support. She could get her cake and eat it too. She's too careful about that. He should know, they were together for almost a decade.

Ryan's thoughts are racing at the speed of sound. An epiphany. Maybe he should really try to hook up with my brother. Hell, they both live in Florida, albeit hundreds of miles and substantial lifestyles apart. What better time? It will give Ryan an excuse to be A.W.O.L. for a couple of days, although Margaret isn't really a fan of Sean, and she really will not take kindly to them meeting.

Heck, it's a good idea.

CHAPTER NINE

The difference in weather between Central Florida and South Florida is like leaving New York and flying to New Orleans. The steam bath effect. While the temperatures may be the same, the humidity is the x factor. Miami is the same way. Also, Miami is now so much different from the rest of Florida that you think you may need a passport. Kind of like a real-life Disney World.

Getting a residential address from his brother is harder than pulling teeth. Sean has always been secretive, but this is ridiculous. If anything ever happened to him, how would Ryan know where he lived? That's how he wants it. Ryan reflects that Sean's precautions have more to do with his safety than with his privacy. Ryan wrestles with the possibility that he should probably listen to Margaret and wash his hands of him, but he just simply can't.

He arrives at the restaurant in South Beach a few minutes before the time they had agreed to meet and is seated at a nice outside table by a waitperson wearing practically nothing at all. People watching is fantastic. It is a cross between the characters from the bar scene in the first *Star*

Wars movie and *La La Land*. Ryan is awakened from his daydream by a hand on his shoulder. His twin brother has somehow entered the restaurant without being seen—by Ryan at least.

"Let's go inside. It's more private. I have a table," Sean whispers. He leads, Ryan follows.

Once seated in a dark, freezing corner of the restaurant, Ryan asks, "What the hell is going on?"

"Sometimes it's better to be safe than sorry."

Now, that was enlightening. "Why all the cloak and dagger stuff?"

"My business is expanding too fast for some of the old guard. They're demanding I respect them more . . . like before."

A drip of sweat slides down Ryan's back. This reunion is not turning out as expected. "How have you been? It sounds like things are going great."

"Ryan, for our entire lives we have sought the same goal but have approached getting there in very different ways. I think that things are now positioned for me so that I can make decisions from the right side of the fence for a change. I need a little help with technical matters, however," Sean states not making eye contact with his brother, a fact Ryan notes. It always indicates that whatever follows will be either dangerous or illegal or most likely—both.

"What can I do for you?" Ryan asks.

"I need to set up a Panamanian corporation so I can transfer funds into a Grand Cayman account from which I can continue to send you weekly deposits."

"You may be my brother, but I am not going to get involved with anything that even seems like money laundering." *This does not sound good at all.*

"No . . . it isn't like that. The corporation is needed so that I can register vessels in Panama. Freighters that will operate in the Caribbean. Completely legit. I have spent a lot of time researching the market."

Is his brother going straight, or does he have a hidden agenda? "What experience do you have?"

"Plenty. And I have contacts for everyone needing bulk goods shipped throughout the Caribbean."

"I do not have experience in this type of business and if you think it is sound . . . you have my blessings. I can send you the names of several people who specialize in offshore accounts. As long as the deposits into your account are as before, I will continue to invest them." Ryan is satisfied with his response.

"Great, let's order lunch. My treat."

The next hour passes quickly and pleasantly. The brothers chat about everything and nothing. It is pleasant enough, but superficial. Ryan harbors grave concerns about Sean's enterprise and the people with whom he has been associating—and those with whom he may be associating in the future.

On the drive back to Orlando, Ryan finds himself torn. Should he tell Margaret he went to Miami to meet with Sean or simply say nothing? He chooses the latter. *Let sleeping dogs lie.*

Ryan is tormented. Traffic sucks and requires him to concentrate, while the feeling in the pit of his stomach is tearing him apart. Ryan decides that he should simply handle his brother like any other client, wait until the divorce is final and try to work through where his relationship with Margaret is going.

And so . . . the next year passes. Sean sends a check each week; Judith and Ryan are divorced without further ado thanks in part to the technical expertise of Stephen; and he and Margaret are doing well together—until.

CHAPTER TEN

At about ten o'clock in the morning, Margaret rushes into Ryan's office. The two of them had arrived, together, as they almost always do, about an hour earlier after a very pleasant breakfast at a new café that has just opened. The weather forecast is a Chamber of Commerce special: high in the upper 70s with low humidity. What can go wrong?

"Ryan, two agents from the FBI are in the reception area. They want to talk with you. I asked them what they wanted to discuss, and they said *Sean*. That was all the information they provided except that they showed me their credentials. I called Stephen and he is on line two. What the hell is going on?"

"I have no idea. Offer them coffee and put them in a conference room. Then, tell them I will join them in ten minutes. I want to ask Stephen a couple of things. And Margaret, thanks for being so efficient." Ryan grabs the phone and says, a bit louder than necessary, "Stephen, the feds are here and want to talk to me about Sean. What should I say?"

"As little as possible. Listen Ryan, this is important; under no circumstance should you volunteer any information. Ask if they have any paperwork. Ask if you are in any way involved in their inquiry. If they say *no,* tell them to put it in writing, which I will review and then we can schedule a meeting. If they are seeking any documents, they will need a court order. Got it?"

"Shit."

"I take that as a yes. Call me when they leave."

"Thanks, Stephen."

Ryan finds his knees a little shaky when he stands to go to the conference room. He breathes deeply—twice and walks toward the lion's den.

Both agents quickly rise when Ryan enters the room. Each offers their hand to shake while producing their IDs in the other hand. Although one of the agents is about Ryan's size and age, the other is a young woman with close cropped red hair and very green eyes.

"Good morning," the male agent begins. "My name is Stephen Tanner, and my partner is Anne Dylan. We are from the Miami Regional office and want to ask you some questions about your brother, Sean."

"My attorney told me to ask you if I am in any way an object of your inquiry." Ryan's voice is surprisingly firm.

"Not at this time and under these circumstances," Agent Tanner replies.

"Then our interview is over until my attorney is available. Shall I call him now and check his schedule?"

Both FBI agents appear to be taken aback by Ryan's response, which may be attributed to the fact that most people they interview are so scared of the FBI. that they will say anything to get rid of the agents.

"Yes, please," Agent Dylan answers. "We can schedule a meeting on Monday or Tuesday next week either here or in Miami at our offices." Her voice is cold as ice.

"I will call Attorney Blackman and ask him which date is convenient and I will call you with a firm date and time," Ryan replies staring straight at the agent.

Agent Dylan stares directly back at Ryan. "Here is my card with my direct number. If neither date is good, please give me several alternative times." The FBI agent brusquely extends his hand.

"I will call you to let you know as soon as I reach Attorney Blackman. Let me show you out." Ryan opens the conference room door and walks across the reception area to the oak doors emblazoned with brass letters announcing where they are *Simpson, Tucker*.

"I look forward to our next meeting. Sorry to barge in on you without warning." Agent Tanner is trying to sound sincere.

"No problem," Ryan insists, although it will soon to be a real problem—a real big problem.

Margaret intercepts Ryan as he returns to his office. "What was that all about?"

"I'm not really sure. They want to talk to me about Sean, but they didn't say anything substantive. I called Stephen and he told me that I say as little as possible. I informed the agents that I was not prepared to speak with them without counsel. They seemed to understand, although I bet they thought they could intimidate me. After the go-round we had with the SEC a couple of years ago, the less said the better. These guys spend most of their time on fishing expeditions. They don't know anything and want people like me to help them do whatever it is they are doing."

"Ryan, that's pretty cavalier. It's the FBI and not some junior staff attorney from the SEC who didn't even understand that we were not market makers, but simply advisors who have been in business for a long time with an impeccable track record."

"The theory is the same. These guys run around looking for problems rather than solving obvious existing problems. They don't want to do the leg work . . . the research. They want to throw everything against the wall and see what sticks, who they can trap and screw over. They have neither a conscience nor any oversight."

"Wow! What started that diatribe?" Margaret slowly shakes her head.

"I don't like them bursting into my office, without any authority, to ask me questions about my brother. If they want answers to questions about Sean, they should find him and ask him . . . not me." Ryan is getting more than a little hot under the collar.

"That's not the way it works. They want to gather facts and if the facts show Sean did something wrong, which more than likely he has, then they will go after him . . . not the other way around."

"Margaret, what's with the snide remark about Sean? Neither of us knows anything about what he does and I for one want to keep it that way."

"Sorry. I guess your brother rubs me the wrong way. He is so secretive. It's spooky. Look, call Stephen, and work out the logistics of meeting with those folks. The sooner this is over, the better you will feel. The feds make everyone nervous and maybe a little angry because they seem to be in every corner of your life. Theoretically, they are trying to keep us safe. From what and from whom is a bit confusing, however. Let's leave early and go a movie. The weather forecast is for showers." Margaret is trying to sound conciliatory.

"Thanks. I love you." Ryan wraps his arms around Margaret.

CHAPTER ELEVEN

Ryan and Stephen agree that Tuesday would be the day for the FBI interview. Stephen will fly down from Boston on Monday afternoon and the two will go over strategy for the meeting. Although Ryan and Margaret are a number, they both think it best for each to have their own homes. Ryan is not totally sure why Margaret is so adamant, but he has to admit that he likes his private time.

Stephen opts to rent a car since he has an elderly aunt still living in Central Florida who he wants to see after their meeting. The two friends spent most of the evening catching up, rather than planning for the meeting. They know so little about what the feds are looking for, they decide to enjoy each other's company. Stephen proudly tells Ryan that although his golf game is suffering, he would never consider giving up coaching Little League.

They drive to Ryan's office early the next morning, well in advance of the 9:30 meeting. Stephen emphasizes the need to listen rather than speak, which is fine with Ryan, who has a very uneasy feeling. He knows that he has not done anything even remotely illegal, but he is not so sure about Sean.

"What if they ask whether Sean has an account here at the firm?" Ryan asks.

"The answer is yes. Let them ask follow up questions. Do not answer more than is absolutely required." Stephen's answer makes sense.

There is a sharp knock on the door, followed by Margaret walking in. "They're here. They have a stenographer with them. Does that mean anything, Stephen?"

"It means they want to concentrate on their questions more than on Ryan's answers."

"I don't understand," Ryan interjects.

"These folks think there is a lot of ground to cover, and very little time. So, it makes sense that they ask all the questions they need and read your answers later. This is not cross examination where the answer might lead to a new question. They are clearly in the early stages of investigating whatever they are investigating. Let's go."

"Maybe we should have Margaret bring in a steno pad and be our stenographer." Ryan is serious.

"Actually, if you don't mind playing the role of a beautiful secretary, it might just rattle them a bit."

"Let's go!" Margaret rises and leads Ryan and Stephen to the conference room, stopping to grab a pad and two pens off a nearby desk.

The agents reacted exactly as Stephen had predicted. Margaret's presence flusters Agents Tanner and Dylan.

"I thought this is to be an interview with Mr. McCallum and counsel," Ms. Dylan stammers.

"So did we, but since you brought in a stenographer, we decided to do the same." There is a sense of satisfaction on Stephen's face. Score one for the good guys.

"Where's her machine?" Agent Tanner inserts.

"Old school," Margaret defiantly replies.

"Shall we begin?" Stephen asks rhetorically.

"Do you want me to swear in the witness?" asks the FBI stenographer.

"It is my understanding that this is an informal interview. If I am mistaken, then we can end right now, and I will await a subpoena." Stephen's voice is menacingly lower.

"No! No! There is no need to swear in Mr. McCallum," sputters Agent Tanner. Agent Dylan resumes her icy stare, without effect.

"Please begin," Attorney Blackman is all business and Ryan loves it.

Agent Dylan opens a pad not dissimilar from the one Margaret is holding. "For the record, is Sean McCallum your brother?"

I look at Stephen, who nods. "Yes." I answer.

"When is the last time you saw him?"

"Why?" I blurt out.

"Ryan, just answer the questions until I tell you not to." Stephen sounds somewhat reassuring.

"A little over a year ago," I reply. Heeding Stephen's earlier advice I did not say where.

"Where did you meet?"

At this rate of inquiry, we will be here all day. "We met at a small restaurant in South Beach for lunch. I do not remember the name of the place or what I ate."

"Please tell us what he said to you and what you said to him."

"Agent Dylan, if you provide me with a non-prosecution agreement, I will instruct Mr. McCallum to answer." Stephen extends his hand in anticipation of being handed the document he has requested.

"I am not sure whether your client is involved with his brother's business dealings, which we are investigating," the agent replies.

"Without the agreement, this, and all subsequent interviews have concluded." Stephen starts to put his pad and pencils into his briefcase.

"No! Wait! We do not believe your client is in any way involved, but we have to make sure," Agent Dylan sputters.

"I sleep better at night knowing the FBI is investigating malfeasance, but without the agreement, you will have to do so without Mr. McCallum's assistance."

The agents look at each other, not happily. Stephen has turned the tables. Usually, the feds use the NPA as a carrot to coerce cooperation. Now they are confronted with a different landscape—no NPA—no cooperation. Agent Tanner pulls out some papers from his briefcase and with great trepidation hands them to Stephen.

"A non-prosecution agreement signed by the deputy director," he says.

"This might be a good time for a lunch break so that I can read over the agreement. Is a half hour sufficient?" Stephen is not cutting these guys any slack.

"There is a great deli next door," Margaret adds.

"Thanks." Agent Dylan tries to sound upbeat, but it is obvious that she is very unhappy.

Ryan holds the door open for the departing agents and the bewildered stenographer. "Now that went well," he says to Stephen and Margaret.

"Don't get too excited. You were never a target. They undoubtedly know that you and Sean are not really close. I am sure they have him under surveillance. You two go out and please bring me an unsweetened iced tea while I read this epistle." Stephen smiles.

CHAPTER TWELVE

The feds return in less than twenty minutes, *ready for bear*, as they say, but neither Ryan nor Stephen even rise when they return.

"Agent Tanner, you don't expect me to have my client sign this agreement, do you? I must admit it is a nice touch to have it already signed by the Deputy Director, but it is woefully inadequate and provides very few safeguards for Mr. McCallum. I have taken the liberty of drafting a revised, substantially shorter agreement. If you call assistant Attorney General Christine Wheeler, I am sure she will approve the form of the NPA and authorize either of you to sign the same on behalf of the Bureau. She and I have had numerous cases together and we have come to an understanding that *less is often more* in this type of agreement. I have her direct phone number if you need it. Oh, don't forget to mention that it's the same agreement we used in the *Costina* case."

The sound of a pin dropping would deafen the room. Agent Dylan tries to pull herself together. "Yes, if you have her direct number that would be helpful. Can we use another room to call her?"

"Please stay here. We can go back to Mr. McCallum's office. You'll need to dial extension eighteen from the phone on the sideboard to get an outside line." Margaret turns and walks toward the conference room door. Stephen and Ryan quickly follow.

"I am impressed," Ryan says. "Really impressed."

Stephen shrugs. "It's what I do old buddy. It's what I do. I am off to visit the men's room."

"Ryan, what exactly is happening? I mean with Sean," Margaret asks impatiently.

"I am not totally sure, but it seems like my dear brother is up to no good," Ryan answers.

"Are you going to tell them about his account?"

"Only if I am asked and if Stephen thinks I should." It is clear that Ryan's reply does not comfort Margaret.

"You need to distance yourself as much as possible from him," Margaret says.

"We really aren't that close," Ryan responds.

"Bull shit! You'd walk the plank for him, although I cannot fathom why." Margaret tone sounds entirely too sharp to Ryan. Sharp and uncaring.

"He is my brother. Don't you understand?"

"What I understand is that you have worked your ass off all your life without Sean and have accomplished a great deal. Don't be blinded by your mutual DNA. He is a crook, gangster, thug . . ."

Ryan holds up his hand like a traffic cop. "Margaret, drop it! You don't understand. You couldn't understand. I have always kept whatever Sean does at arm's length. I know nothing. I don't want to know anything. Leave it at that. I will answer their questions honestly, but I will not do anything to help them. If he has done something wrong, the FBI doesn't need my help."

"What do you mean . . . something?"

Before Ryan answers, Stephen walks into the office. "Time to see how our fine feathered friends are doing. I want to finish this by five and it's nearly two already.

The threesome returns to the conference room and knock but immediately enter, not waiting for an answer.

"How are we doing?" Stephen asks.

"Ms. Wheeler said that your draft was fine. She authorized me to sign on behalf of the Bureau. She also said she would e-mail you a confirmation of authority." Agent Tanner is not a happy camper. As he firmly signs the NPA, Stephen's cell phone vibrates. He looks at the screen.

"Assistant Attorney General Wheeler is very efficient. I have her authority confirmation. So, let's pick up where we ended before lunch."

A much-rattled Agent Dylan begins. "You said that you last saw your brother in Miami a little over a year ago, correct?"

"Yes, that is correct."

"Do you speak by phone?"

"Yes."

"When is the last time you and he spoke by phone?"

"On December 24 at about 6 o'clock."

"How is it you remember the call with such precision?" Agent Dylan thinks she is on a roll.

"Because Sean always calls me on Christmas eve at about 6 in the evening. Every year for as long as I can remember. Ever since high school."

Agent Dylan's eyes narrow. "Can you remember when he called you before the Christmas Eve call?"

"Yes."

Agent Dylan looks triumphant. "When was that?"

"The preceding Christmas Eve," Ryan answers.

"Do you mean you only talk to your brother by phone on Christmas Eve?"

"Yup."

Trying to regroup, the flustered agent asks, "When did you last see your brother prior to meeting him for lunch about a year ago?"

"At least ten years ago. He didn't even attend my wedding." Ryan's voice has an edge to it.

"Is it fair to say that you and your brother do not have a close relationship?"

"It would certainly seem so." Ryan casts a glance at Margaret who is sitting stoically across the table. "It would certainly seem so."

"I can't think of anything else. Oh wait, do you have his address?"

"I have a post office box number for him in Palm Beach. I have never received any mail from him . . . ever. Not even a birthday card."

"Do you have the P.O. box number?" Agent Dylan is relentless but getting nowhere.

"Yes, I actually put it in my phone a couple of years ago when I upgraded my cell service." Ryan retrieves the phone from his pocket and pushes keys allowing him to access his e-phone book. He turns the phone so that the screen is facing the two agents, who promptly write down the address.

"Do you have a phone number for your brother?" Agent Tanner asks.

"No. My only contact information for my brother is that which I just showed you," Ryan answers.

"Thank you for consenting to the interview. May we have a copy of the NPA signed by Mr. McCallum for our records?' Agent Dylan is quite a bit less formidable now than she was a couple of hours ago.

Stephen gives Ryan the agreements, already signed by Agent Tanner, and a pen. "Sign here." Ryan does so and one fully executed agreement is given to the waiting agent and the other is put into Stephen's briefcase. Everyone rises, exchanges handshakes and—it's over.

Stephen looks at his watch and says, "I timed this pretty well. I'm booked on the 6:40 and will be home in Boston by 9 and have an hour to see my Aunt Ruth. Not too shabby. Margaret, don't let him get into any trouble . . . maybe I should say more trouble." He gives Ryan a light punch on the arm and blows Margaret a kiss. Stephen gives a slight wave as he turns and walks out the door.

"We need to talk," Margaret says. "You conveniently didn't mention that you have almost $4,000,000 in Sean's account."

"They didn't ask."

"I know, but don't you think it might be important?"

"If they're looking into Sean's financial life, let them. If they want to schedule another interview because they've dug up something, I am sure Stephen will say the same thing. I told the truth, regardless of whether I was under oath or not. The transcript will show they never asked me about Sean's finances. So why are you mad? I did everything to the letter."

"Yes, but you were not forthright."

"Do you mean like volunteering information about my brother to law enforcement? No way. That's their job. I did mine as a good citizen and cooperated."

Margaret paces back and forth. "Sean may be your brother, but he is a crook and based on some of the things you have told me, he is violent and basically amoral."

"He is my brother and that is the end of the story. Period. He should not be a source of conflict between us."

"I agree that he shouldn't be a source of conflict, but your blind loyalty to him is neither deserved nor right."

"He is my brother."

"Ryan, if you aren't prepared to be honest, maybe I'll have to be."

"Margaret, what the hell are you talking about? This is not your issue, it's mine. Don't get involved."

"I am involved. I am going home. If you want to talk, let me know. Margaret opens the office door and marches down the corridor.

CHAPTER THIRTEEN

Ryan alternates between fear, anger, and sorrow. His emotions crash into him from all directions—taking his breath away. He is confused and conflicted. All he knows is that he has got to get away from Margaret's house. Not run away, but merely create a space so that he can think. Maybe a road trip is the answer. Ryan's cognitive processes are not fully functional. He needs to get back to his place so he can think. Should he call the police and explain what happened? Would they believe him? He has already moved Margaret's lifeless body. They'll figure out that she didn't drown. So, why did he do that? Guilt? What would a good prosecutor say? If you are innocent and it was an accident, why did you move the body and not call 911? An alibi won't cut it. Ingrid knows he was there. But maybe he can say that when he left, she was fine. Angry at him, but alive.

The ride back into town is without incident. Ryan's pulse slows, which mentally helps his ability to concentrate on his problem. Call Stephen. That's the answer.

He speed dials his friend's number and hears the recorded sound of Stephen's voice mail. "Stephen . . . Ryan.

Sorry to bother you after your fantastic performance today, but something has just come up . . . and it is really important. Call anytime. It's about Margaret. Thanks." Voice mail is so frustrating.

As he eases the Mercedes into its parking space under his condominium complex, Ryan has an epiphany. Call Sean. Who has more experience about these things than anyone else Ryan knows? That's it, call Sean. Tell him everything. Drive down to Miami and meet him in person. How to get in touch with his brother is the problem. He was asked if he had Sean's phone number and he said that he didn't, which is technically correct. Ryan suddenly activates his cell and starts to scroll. Easy, just look for December 24th calls. Bingo! Unknown caller with a Palm Beach area code. Provided Sean hasn't swapped out his phone, he might be able to make contact.

Ryan pushes the return call button. The phone rings about six times before a recording asks him to leave a message. "Sean, it's Ryan. Please call. Thanks" Another damn voice mailbox. Other than pouring single malt on the rocks; all Ryan can do is patiently wait until either Stephen or Sean calls.

However, Ryan has never been known for his patience and one single malt turns into two and then three, so by the time Stephen calls, Ryan is sound asleep. His message simply says he is returning Ryan's call and that he has to be in Court in the morning, but will call back after 1 pm. Sean's return call comes significantly later. His message simply says that he'll call again first thing in the morning—whatever that means.

Considering that he had three drinks on an empty stomach, Ryan does not feel that bad the next morning.

Then everything hits like a proverbial rogue wave. The local TV news initially reports Margaret's death as accidental. The police spokesperson says that the victim appears to have tripped over some pots on the pool deck, hit her head and tumbled into the water. The medical examiner's office is trying to ascertain time of death, but it was estimated to be early evening. After listening to several different stations, Ryan has a brilliant idea. Well, *brilliant* might not be the right word, but the idea is nevertheless the best way he may be able to save his precious skin. He calls the Orlando Police Department headquarters and asks to speak with the officer investigating the death of Margaret Adams.

After a moment or so, a voice answers, "This is Detective Michael Polski, how may I help you?"

"Good morning Detective, my name is Ryan McCallum, and I am . . . was a friend of Margaret Adams and I just saw on the news that she had an accident and died. I wanted to offer whatever help your office might need. To cut to the chase, Margaret worked with me, and we were very close. In fact, I was over at her house last night for a glass of wine."

"What time was that Mr. McCallum?"

"I arrived about six thirty . . . twenty 'til seven. It was getting dark. We had had a long day at the office, and she asked if I would like to come over for a drink." Ryan's voice remains strong.

"When did you leave?"

"A little before eight. I was exhausted. As I said it was a long day. I went home, had a drink, and went to bed." So far so good.

"Is there any way you can verify anything you just told me?"

"What part?" Ryan is getting a little nervous.

"Let's start with arrival time and departure time." Detective Polski is very matter of fact.

"Actually, right after I arrived, a friend of Margaret's called, and I heard her say that I had just arrived."

"Do you know her name?"

"She said it was Ingrid. I assume that it was her friend Ingrid Sorenson. I imagine that Margaret's caller ID would have a time and I am sure Ingrid can confirm their conversation."

"Okay. Can you confirm that you left around 8 PM and went to your home?"

"I made a call to a friend shortly after I got home, but he didn't answer so I left a voice message."

"What is your friend's name and number?"

"His name is Stephen Blackman. He's my attorney with whom Margaret and I had been in a meeting all day. I wanted to thank him for his counsel."

"What was the nature of the meeting and with whom?"

"Two FBI agents wanted to ask me questions about my brother, who I think they are investigating. Since I rarely speak to him, I was of little help."

"Where was Ms. Adams when you left her home around 8 pm?"

"She was standing next to the sliding glass doors leading to the pool. We had had a bit of a disagreement and I decided to leave, besides which I was tired. I knew that our disagreement could be smoothed over in the morning but it could explode if I stayed and we continued bickering. This morning, while getting ready to leave for the office I heard of the accident on the news and since I may have been the last person to see her, I thought I should call."

"It is always better to come forward with information than to have us later discover the information and wonder why you didn't tell us in the first place. I am going to prepare a summary of our conversation and ask you if I can send it to you for review. Are you free later today? I will need some additional information from you especially regarding Ms. Adam's friends and family, the contact information for Attorney Blackman and a bit more detail of your meeting with the FBI."

"Detective Polski, if you can send over your notes for me to review by noon, I will review them and get back to you by 2 and assuming everything is ready to go, if you can come to my office between 4 and 5, I will gladly sign the witness statement."

"That is fine. What is your address?"

"I am in the Sunshine Bank and Trust Building 17th floor."

"I will email you the notes. Do you have a personal email account rather than the office?"

"Yes . . . and thank you. My email address is ryanm at expressmail dot net.

"Thanks. See you this afternoon." Detective Polski said as she hung up.

Ryan is pleased with himself. The perfect deflection. Admit everything the cops could figure out anyway and it looks like you have nothing to hide. Ryan then makes a poor choice. He decides not to tell Stephen the story behind the story. Be cooperative with law enforcement and show an appropriate amount of grief, which won't be an act, and everything will be as it appears—a tragic accident, which it really was.

CHAPTER FOURTEEN

Sean's journey during the last two decades has led him to a very different place. While still in high school, before he dropped out, Sean ran errands for a couple of local *wise guys*. Basically, he had become a private courier service. He would pick up and deliver small packages throughout the Heights and neighboring environs. Sean was reliable and more importantly, he never asked what was in the parcels he delivered. One thing led to another and soon Sean was doing small tasks for the bosses in Boston's North End. It was a significant promotion since being Irish was a real disadvantage in the world in which he is now employed. Sean's reputation for efficiency and keeping his mouth shut gains him the attention of some very influential people, who were looking for some new blood in the organization. It didn't hurt that Sean was good with his fists.

Although Sean's academic credentials were less than outstanding, his talent to acquire knowledge orally serves him well. He works hard to learn languages, first Italian, the primary language of his employers, then Spanish which is quickly becoming the *lingua franca* of the under world.

He soon has basic conversational skills in both Mandarin and Cantonese which are unheard of in Sean's circle of acquaintances. It proves to be very useful that Sean is able to understand others speaking in their native tongues. He never tries to show off and keeps his knowledge a secret. It is a gift well used, especially when his employers are saying things they do not want to share with Sean.

Sean's money management style differs significantly from that of his twin brother. He becomes a *debt collector,* and he employs many creative ways to get the debts paid. New England mob friction between the larger Italian faction of the mob and the closer-knit Irish faction almost breaks out into a full-scale war. Sean is uniquely situated. He is employed by the Italians but is Irish through and through. He starts to broker small deals with each side profiting quite handsomely. The two groups quickly realize that working together is far more lucrative than fighting, although generations of distrust still make it difficult. Sean becomes the man in the middle. Both sides trust him and are quick to recognize the importance of his rising stature.

For about five years everything goes smoothly. Although the deals Sean puts together are relatively small, they are well thought out and equally well executed, in one sense of the word. Whenever a young rising star gets the attention of the folks at the top, a lot of folks at the bottom become jealous.

One day in late September, Sean and a couple of *associates* go to visit the owner of a dry-cleaning supply company. The man has been a regular customer and makes his protection payments like clockwork. When Sean asks for his monthly stipend, the owner says he paid it yesterday.

"Why'd you do that?" Sean asks.

"The guy told me that you were out of town and that he would be handling some of your accounts. He used your name, so I figured it was legit. He was with a couple of guys who were obviously packing. So . . . what was I to do?"

Sean thought for a moment and then asks, "Was the guy a Dago or a Mick?"

"Actually, he looked like the basic all-American type. He was about six foot tall with brown hair, cut short, like the military. Nothing distinguishing except that his eyes were not both the same color. Not really different, but enough for me to remember."

"What about the other two goons?"

"Could have been anyone, except they also had crew cuts and nicely tailored suits. Expensive. And nice shoes."

"Other than asking you for payment, did he say anything else? Did he have any accent?"

"He said *thank you* and *I'll see you next month.* Then he said *I'll give Sean your regards.* That was strange because I have never mentioned our relationship to anyone. You know, as I remember, he did have a slight accent. It wasn't Italian, it was like Russian. Very slight, like when he said *thank you* it sounded like *dank you.*"

"Mr. Adelman, you did okay. I will follow up. Do you think you could identify the man if you saw a photograph?"

"Unless it was a color close up, probably not. It was his eyes that made him different, but I will help if I can."

"Thank you and please don't give any money to anyone but me." Sean nods at his two companions, and they all leave the building quickly.

"What was that all about?" One of the men asks.

"Someone is trying to move in on us. I bet he has been following us for a while and paying our people a visit just before we are scheduled to arrive. We have quite a bit of ground to cover."

And cover it he did. After meeting with his employers in Boston, he is told to go to Providence and check with the patriarch. Sean's reputation precedes him, and he is put in charge of a task force to get to the bottom of the problem. Sean applies several of his many skills; initially acquiring the rudiments of the Russian language. After three weeks, the Russian problem is solved, and several bodies lay at the bottom of Narraganset Bay. The nascent attempt of the Russian mob to take over certain business interests is stifled, and Sean gets a promotion.

In all matters relating to the mob, or *familia* as it is called by insiders, being *made* is akin to becoming a knight in medieval days, although much more difficult if you are an Irish kid. Sean's ceremony is a graduation of sorts, although he decides not to invite his brother to attend.

Sean is given a very important and lucrative assignment—South Florida. He is to make sure deliveries are handled efficiently and without loss. Several groups have been trying to usurp the mob's territory, but they did not expect a Spanish speaking, Irish enforcer to interfere. Sean's religious training comes in handy as he recalls a parable that says: *to kill a snake, one must cut off his head.* The context is not exactly the same, but the effect of eliminating several members of both the Columbian and Mexican cartels within a month of his arrival in sunny Miami has a significant impact. A peace conference is called, and the warring factions meet. The get-together is presided over by the patriarch from Providence, who asks Sean to sit at his right during the sessions. Every hour, the meeting adjourns for about five minutes during which time Sean translates any Spanish side conversations to the patriarch. Everyone thinks the hourly breaks are because the older members of the family have to use the facilities, but by eavesdropping, Sean is able to discover that the cartels have joined together, at least temporarily, against the Italians. A plan to abduct the patriarch and attack mob strongholds both fail, and the snake is cut up unto many pieces. This time without mercy.

Sean's role is becoming much more executive and less *hands on*. It is safer for sure, but the lack of action makes Sean bored and cranky. He decides to become intimately familiar with his employer's accounting system, or rather systems. The amounts of money generated are staggering, and Sean decides he should be given a substantially larger piece of the pie. He is torn. Embezzling is not in his nature. He has worked hard to gain the trust of the dons and that is important. So, he asks. Although his request is initially met with a cold silence, within a week he receives an envelope with $9,900 in cash and a note—*if you don't ask, you won't get!* Although the amounts vary somewhat based on cash flow, every week Sean gets an envelope.

Rather than establishing a showy and lavish South Florida lifestyle, Sean starts to consider his future. Thus, his outreach to his brother. A small BMW sedan and a modest condo, near but not on the beach, is more than sufficient for the kid from the Heights. The weekly stipend is invested by Ryan, and it grows. Sean continues to apply his management skills for the interests of his employers, although with decreasing enthusiasm. Occasionally he undertakes a more personal interest in a problem, mostly to keep himself sharp. Nothing is ever intimate, until he finds himself being swept away by the lure of an associate's wife. Sean has always avoided close relationships with women who he considers a major distraction. It is not like he is not without female companionship, but the superficiality suits him well. He is never tempted to show off his power and wealth. All that changes when Señora Alverez enters his life.

It is all very innocent—so it appears. Carlos, her husband, works for Sean in Little Havana—mostly in collections. Although not tall in stature, he is quick with a knife and easily gains the admiration or even better, fear of his customers. Unfortunately, Carlos has an insatiable love of fast cars, which he cannot really afford to own. So, he borrows them. He never trashes or wrecks these cars. Most are usually recovered within less than a day, albeit they are found several hundred miles from where they had been before Carlos starts his joy ride. Carlos makes a bad decision. While driving a Tesla is definitely cool, it is equipped with a GPS tracking/security system. Within seconds of opening the door, Carlos is looking down at the barrel of a large gun in the hands of a very angry owner. Apparently, any unauthorized entry immediately causes a warning signal to be sent to the cell phone of the Tesla's owner. Bad luck. He luckily escapes with only a six-month sentence and no broken bones. Carlos luck changes from bad to good because he cannot be connected to his other thefts. It doesn't hurt that Sean finds him a very well-connected lawyer to cut a deal.

What is a man to do? Sean provides care and comfort for Carlos' wife during his incarceration. Rather than being surreptitious, Sean and the lovely Señora Alverez are seen together on several occasions in public. His thought process has been slightly obscured by his infatuation. He reasons that by appearing in public, people will not gossip that he is secretly having a "thing" with Carlos' wife. He was simply being a good friend by keeping the lonely lady busy. While this theory plays reasonably well with Sean's business colleagues, it does not resonate with the Cuban American community of South Florida. Sean is clueless that others are reacting badly. He does not see or chooses to ignore all of his instincts. The hierarchy of organized crime is not as clearly defined in Florida as it is in New England. Several times Sean finds himself in the cross hairs of some pretty angry friends and family of Carlos Alverez, who is scheduled for early release for good behavior.

Crime in South Florida is about as far from organized as you can get. In the old days, there were clear boundaries regarding both services and territory. Gambling was pretty much under the control of the Jewish syndicate, while enforcement and protection was exclusively Italian. Drugs were pretty much the domain of the large Mexican and Columbian cartels, who fought amongst themselves for control. With the influx of immigrants from Asia, South and Central America, and the rise of the political influence of the Seminole Nation, things began to radically change.

Legislation gave the Seminole Nation a virtual monopoly on gambling in Florida. Although a few gambling outlets remained, the real money is either at the Hard Rock facilities or online sports betting outlets. Protection actually increases in importance since different competing groups are putting the squeeze on merchants. The Italian grasp is weakening. Drugs become the currency of the underworld, along with guns and the importation of non-documented immigrants. Human trafficking is big bucks. The traditional crime elements want nothing to do with the latter.

Asian, South American, and Mexican gangs each vie for a piece of the action. Unlike their predecessors, these new groups are not based on family, but are organized around greed and disdain for the order of things. In-fighting reduces the effectiveness of these groups. Law enforcement is sometimes used as a weapon for gangs. If one group is expecting a shipment of drugs and another group deems that their space is being compromised, DEA is mysteriously notified of both timing and method of shipment. This may be good for law enforcement, but gives rise to violent warfare amongst the competitors, often extending from their place of origin to the streets of almost every big city in America.

In-fighting also costs money. It is inefficient at multiple levels. That is where Sean fits in. He is acknowledged as the voice of reason. His ability to communicate with the different factions, convincing them that there is plenty to go around, slows the aggressive non-profitable segments of the crime world. Guns are separated from drugs as an income source and territories are created. It is almost like political re-districting, but without Gerrymandering. Gambling is all but ignored. Dog racing is banned, and horse racing is losing the aura of the Sport of Kings. Numbers and penny ante gambling is altogether ignored. Collection and protection remain within the purview of the Italian family, but its importance in terms of total dollars is materially less thus reducing the influence of the old guard and diluting the traditional rules of behavior.

Sean's Irish background makes him unique within the South Florida crime world. No one labels him as being for or against any group. He has gradually distanced himself from the family. Sean is becoming increasingly independent. Sean is viewed by the folks in South Florida as having only one goal; maximizing profit and making sure it is distributed to everyone even handedly, including his former employers. His weekly bonus pales in relation to the hundreds of thousands he sends to Providence each month. The money is totally the result of Sean's efforts, which include almost daily meetings between the differing factions in order to make sure everything is *on the table*. Rather than be underhanded, he simply tells his former employers that he is wants to assume a new role: a consultant to the underworld. Since the system Sean has installed is working so well, he is afforded the opportunity to withdraw from the organization's affairs, an opportunity that is virtually never granted. Peace and profit prevail until Carlos Alverez is released.

CHAPTER FIFTEEN

S ean does not really have time to deal with Carlos
Alverez. As far as Sean is concerned, although
he admits that Señora Alverez was very alluring,
business comes first. He does not want to create a
rift between the various factions in the community. The
explanation that he was simply trying to keep Carolos'
wife busy and *out of trouble* while Alverez was in jail gains
traction with everyone. Everyone except Carlos.

The rumors of being a marked man do not phase Sean
in the least. He is far too important in South Florida's
underworld. He makes everyone a lot of money, and everyone knows it and they go to great lengths to stick up for
Sean and cover his back. Everyone except Carlos Alverez.

When Ryan and Sean finally connect, Sean suggests
that his brother visit him for a little deep-sea fishing, a
little bar hopping and a little . . . whatever. Since Ryan
has already laid the groundwork with Detective Polski, he
is confident that the entire tragic episode will gradually
go away. However, in the spirit of continued cooperation,
Ryan takes the initiative.

"Detective Polski?" Ryan asks.

"Yes."

"This is Ryan McCallum. I am not nagging you about the investigation but rather I want to tell you that I am going to be out of town for about ten days. I thought it would look bad if you tried to reach me and found out that I had left the city. If you need me for any reason, either call my cell phone or leave a message at my office. I will be checking in pretty much every day."

"May I ask where you are going?"

"I'm going to South Florida and try my hand offshore fishing," Ryan answers. He omits that he is seeing Sean.

"Good luck and thank you for calling. I wish all people of interest in a potential homicide case were as cooperative. Give me a call when you return to Orlando." Detective Polski breaks the connection.

Although the phrase, *people of interest* is a bit off putting, Ryan is pleased with himself. He still hasn't talked to Stephen, but that might not be necessary. Well, maybe he should tell Stephen what happened. He didn't do anything wrong, except kind of tampering with evidence by moving Margaret's body. He will omit that point. Most of his brokerage accounts can be handled by his assistants, although whenever he went on business trips before, he always had Margaret watching over everything.

He tries Stephen's office but is told that he is on trial in Portland, Maine and won't be back until the end of the week. Ryan elects not to bother calling his friend on his cell phone. Ryan is only going to be away for a week or so. What could possibly happen? What indeed?

Sean is both surprised and thrilled that Ryan is going to travel to South Florida to visit. Sean also seriously needs a break. There is a chilling sense of tension in the air.

Carlos Alverez is shooting off his mouth and Sean does not like the attention that he is getting. If you say something enough times and with enough conviction, people will believe you, especially if there is more than a grain of truth to the rumors. Sean does not feel threatened personally, but Carlos' theatrics are affecting business. Everyone wants to know; *Was it true? Were you fooling around with his wife? Aren't you going to shut him up?*

The inquiries are becoming tedious. A couple of folks even decide they don't want to do business with Sean any more. And the family isn't thrilled either. If Sean becomes the source of unrest his real usefulness as a peacekeeper and a deal maker measurably wanes.

Needless to say, Ryan does not know any of this when he makes plans to head to South Florida. He is hoping to catch some rays and some fish and reconnect with his twin. He is also hoping that the Margaret issue will grow old and stale and be chalked up as an accident, albeit a tragic accident. Why did Margaret have to insert herself between the brothers. It was neither something that affected her nor was it any of her business. Why?

"What's done is done," Ryan mumbles to himself.

He quickly snaps out of his pondering and re-enters reality. Analysis has always been Ryan's strength, whether it is a trading decision or a golf swing. Nothing is left to chance. The devil is in the details. He decides that he needs to meticulously review everything that has happened and try to see if there is anything that makes him vulnerable. By putting himself in the other person's shoes, Ryan is able to get perspective. Only one question remains unresolved: how did Margaret's body get into the pool? Since she was dead before he rolled her lifeless body into the water, the medical examiner will quickly ascertain that she did not drown.

"Why am I beating myself up? It's not my issue. I told the police detective that she was fine when I left. I have no idea how she fell or ended up in the pool. Just don't think about it. It will go away. Right?" Ryan decides that talking to himself is not the healthiest thing to do. Call Sean, make travel arrangements and go. Sounds like a plan.

Ryan dials his brother's cell phone. *"Miami . . . here I come!"*

CHAPTER SIXTEEN

S ean is really looking forward to seeing his twin brother. Their lives have basically drifted apart and the opportunity to get together is long overdue. Sean doesn't know much about Margaret other than she and Ryan are very close. All that is about to change.

Ryan's drive from Orlando to Miami takes a little over four hours even traveling on both the Florida Turnpike and then Interstate 95. That's how bad traffic has gotten in the last decade. It used to be a very easy and relaxing three and a half hours, but now, the drivers are crazy. Between cars exceeding 90 miles per hour, overloaded trucks, lost tourists, and roads decaying from over-use and under-maintenance, the ride is definitely a white-knuckle event. There may be some relief in sight if people start using the high speed rail service between Miami and Orlando, but people in Florida seem to be inordinately attached to their cars so behavioral patterns are unlikely to change.

Sean is being his typically secretive self. He doesn't give Ryan his residential address. He simply identifies a place where they will meet. Rather than presuming that Sean might have secured lodging, Ryan makes reservations at a very funky South Beach hotel. The view of the street is terrific and so is the view of the ocean. Ryan opts to shower and change before walking to the designated restaurant. He hopes that his brother has made some kind of plans for fishing.

Dodging roller blading beauties in bikinis has become an art form in South Beach, but Ryan finds it somehow invigorating compared to the stuffy coat and tie world in which he lives.

"Howdy stranger," Sean calls from across the street. One would think that wearing pink shorts with a black tank-top would make the wearer stand out in a crowd, but not in South Beach.

"If I can get across the street without being run down, I'll be right there," Ryan shouts in reply.

After several very tricky maneuvers avoiding the mass of humanity occupying every square foot of the sidewalk, road and environs, Ryan reaches his brother.

"Well done. Still the athletic type," Sean quips.

"Nothing prepares you for South Beach. Let's grab a bite. I am famished." Ryan wraps his arms around his brother and gives him a hug. No one even blinks. It's South Beach.

"I know of a great seafood joint, but it's across the street." Sean starts to laugh uncontrollably.

"You planned on going there before you conned me into putting my life at risk crossing the street." Ryan also starts to laugh. It feels good. It has been a while since he had a real belly laugh. Quite understandable.

The restaurant marque says that it has the "*BEST SEAFOOD IN FLORIDA*"—a significant achievement.

"Let's find a quiet corner. I need to tell you something really important," Ryan says.

"A corner I can get. Quiet may be a little bit harder, however, no one cares." Sean opens the door.

"I suspect a cold beer is the liquid of choice."

Sean immediately raises two fingers in the direction of the bar. "Done."

"I guess you've been here before," Ryan observes.

"Yeah, a couples of times. Follow me." Sean leads his brother to the back of the restaurant, greeting folks along the way.

Before they sit, a waitress, wearing as little as legally allowable, places two beers in koozies on the table.

"You are a big shot, aren't you?"

"Looks are deceiving, bro."

"I'm impressed."

"Coming from you, that is a huge compliment."

"Cheers, Sean." They clink bottles.

"Let's order, then you can tell me what is really on your mind. For years we have both lived in Florida and for years our paths have failed to cross in any meaningful way . . . until now."

Ryan nods.

"What's up?"

"It's a long story."

"I've got the time and the restaurant has a lot of cold beer and some great grilled grouper," Sean offers nonchalantly. Ryan is as tight as a drum.

"Would you all like something to eat?" The waitperson leans over the table as she asks the questions. Sean smiles. Ryan leers.

"Two grilled grouper and grits and two beers when the food is ready." Sean gives his brother a thumbs-up.

"Margaret is dead," Ryan blurts out.

"Whoa! Start from the beginning. And speak slowly. Stick with the facts. I won't interrupt."

"It's a bit complicated," Ryan whines.

"Like I said, I've got the time and the restaurant has the cold beer."

"I'm not sure where to begin," Ryan mutters.

"The beginning is a good place. I'm a good listener."

"Margaret has never been a fan of yours."

"She doesn't even know me! Sorry . . . I said no interruptions."

"She is . . . was convinced that you are a crook and probably a truly bad guy who hangs around with other really bad guys who do some really bad things. She was less than thrilled that I agreed to be your investment advisor. She felt that the money you were sending was tainted. Margaret thought I should send it back. She never understood our relationship." Ryan takes a long drink of beer. He stares at the table for almost a minute.

"Why was it any of her concern in the first place? Sorry, I did it again."

"Good question. Very good question."

The arrival of their food breaks this somber moment. The beers help as well.

"Let's eat before these gorgeous pieces of fish get cold."

"Is there anything else I can get you?" The waitperson asks. Both Ryan and Sean suddenly break out in gales of laughter.

"No thank you. Not now," Sean stutters as he tries to catch his breath.

"Maybe later?"

"We'll let you know. Thanks." Sean stifles a laugh.

The young lady sash shays away.

"Whoa!" Ryan says.

"Welcome to South Beach, kiddo."

CHAPTER SEVENTEEN

The food is superb and the people watching is even better, from Ryan's point of view. Sean fits right in, but a golf shirt with the embroidered name of his club and pressed blue jeans make Ryan stand out as a tourist. A fact that isn't lost on Sean.

"We have to get you something to wear," Sean suggests.

"What's wrong with what I am wearing?"

"Makes you look like a tourist."

"I am a tourist."

"No, you are my guest and some of the places I want to show you are only frequented by locals." Sean has become a fashion maven. Ryan fondly recalls Sean buying him his first blazer a million years ago.

"This place has fantastic food. I'm glad we came here." Ryan is avoiding discussing Margaret.

"Yes it does, but you are trying to avoid telling me about Margaret. So, let's take it from the beginning, bro."

"It's not that simple," Ryan responds.

"And you are not making it any easier."

"I think I need another beer."

Sean raises his hand, and waves to the waitperson who immediately bustles over to their table.

"May we each have another beer and please clear the food dishes. Everything was terrific, especially the service." Sean winks.

"Can we talk here without being overheard?"

"Absolutely. As soon as we get our beer, I want you to tell me what the hell is going on." Sean is rather adamant.

Their drinks arrive. Sean lifts his glass and taps the rim of his brother's beer.

"I want to start at the beginning, but I am not sure where the beginning is. I sense that Margaret always had a level of resentment toward you. Maybe because she felt unable to have the kind of bond we have as twins. I basically ignored it. When you started to send money for me to invest, she started getting high and mighty, but not all the time. I guess the tipping point came when the FBI came to my office."

"The FBI?" Sean shows his first sign of emotion.

"They wanted to interview me but said that I wasn't a target, but you were. Stephen was with me when I was interviewed. I said that we hadn't seen each other in years, and we only spoke once a year on Christmas Eve. I told them that the only address that I have for you is a post box. They were on a fishing expedition and Stephen made them toe the line. I didn't say anything that they didn't already know. They left and that's when Margaret started her preaching to me that I had an obligation to be more forthright with the feds. I told her it was none of her business, but she said that she would turn you in if I didn't. She huffed out of the office. We agreed to get together at her house for a drink and talk this through."

"What did Margaret have against me?" Sean asked.

"Maybe she was jealous, maybe she has a moral compass that says she is always right. I don't know, except that she wouldn't let it go." Ryan takes a long drink of beer.

"Did you meet her that night?"

"Yeah. I went over to her house after I finished at the office. We spent a lot of time together, but she never wanted to live together. I like urban excitement and she likes the more countrified life. When I got there she was still steaming. We had a glass of wine, but she started in on me the second I walked in. She wouldn't back off. I decided to leave. She got up and walked over to the sliders that separate the living room from the pool area. She tripped and fell onto the patio tile. She smacked her head. I ran to see if she was all right, but she was dead. I panicked. I rolled her body into the pool to make it look like an accident. I washed the wine glasses, so it looked like it happened after I left. I tried to reach both you and Stephen but ended up leaving messages. The next morning it was all over the news, and I decided to call the police detective and tell him I was there. I changed the timetable a bit by saying that she was fine when I left, although we had been arguing. I did not mention what we were talking about. I sense that the detective is satisfied and that calling him was a good idea. It made me less of a suspect." Ryan takes another long drink.

"Ryan, Ryan, Ryan. Except for moving the body, it was an accident. The police already know that Margaret was dead before she ended up in the pool. You are their number one suspect."

"What do you mean, *they already know?*" Ryan is clearly rattled.

"Dollars to donuts they performed an autopsy, and they didn't find any water in her lungs which would have been there if she drowned. There's nothing we can do except get a hold of Stephen and tell him the whole thing. The cops don't have a motive. They don't have any proof. Just supposition. Unless there is something more, they don't have enough to take to the State Attorney's office for an indictment. However, if this detective is a persistent SOB, he will be watching you night and day to see if you make a mistake."

"A mistake?"

"Like letting the guilt they instilled in us at St. Mary's over take your common sense. Other than Stephen you are never to say anything to anybody about this. As far as you are concerned this was a terrible accident. Nothing more, nothing less. You cared for Margaret, and this is a personal blow to you, but you had no contributing factor to her death. End of statement."

Ryan nods. Resignation comes with a heavy price tag. He finishes his beer.

So does Sean.

The brothers, so much alike and yet so different, get up. Sean pulls out a $100 bill and puts it on the table. Even in South Florida, that's a lot for a few beers and some fish.

Ryan looks at the money and asks, "are you going to get change?"

"No. I am always seated regardless of the line outside. They have great sea food, and I don't like to wait."

"Makes sense."

"Let's head out and find you some appropriate clothes for South Beach.

CHAPTER EIGHTEEN

Shopping for clothes in South Beach is unlike any clothes shopping Ryan had ever done. It is certainly far different than Harvard Square or, most assuredly, even from the tailor in Orlando who custom makes Ryan's suits. The first obvious distinction is color. Grays, browns, and traditional blacks simply don't exist, except for black underwear. The second obvious distinction is sound. While shopping at a men's clothing store, the sounds are subdued. In South Beach, everything is loud-music, voices, car horns and bicycle bells. Sean guides his brother into a boutique of sorts. The selection is vast, and the clientele certainly make people watching an eye opening experience. Ryan turns as a woman emerges from the dressing room wearing nothing but a tiny bra and thong.

"Which do you like better?" She screams to her companion. "The turquoise or the sea form green?" She holds up one sleeveless shirt and then the other.

"Actually neither." A young man wearing bright red short shorts and a yellow muscle shirt replies.

The young girl walks over to Sean and Ryan and asks their opinion of her choices.

"I think that you would look good in either, but I prefer emerald green to match your eyes. It's the Irish in me." Sean delivers his answer with the touch of a brogue.

"You are a sweetie," the girl says. She leans over and gives Sean a kiss and walks away toward the table on which a pile of sleeveless shirts are piled.

"You are a smooth one, old man. I give you that." Ryan says.

"But of course. When in Rome . . . Let's find you something that doesn't shout *tourist*."

During the next hour, Sean gives his brother a complete makeover. Fortunately, Ryan's routine has always left time for working out, so that he looks rather good in tight tee shirts and a pair of somewhat too snug for his taste, shorts. Flip flops replace his Nike running shoes, and blue tinted wraparound sunglasses finish the new look.

Standing in front of the mirror with Sean next to him, Ryan thinks he is seeing double. The brothers appear so much alike that it's scary.

"Now you fit in," Sean announces. "This calls for a rum and Coke at the dockside. It is the best show in town. I love watching tourists trying to pick up Townies and both trying to figure out the gender of the other."

"I guess everything goes in South Beach, right?" Ryan observes.

"Except when it doesn't" Sean laughs at his response.

"This has promise to be a totally cool day."

The two leisurely stroll toward the docks. The crowd is fascinating, although a bit overwhelming. Sweaty bodies shoulder to shoulder, not really moving. Sean, followed by Ryan, bob and weave through the crowd. No one seems to be going anywhere, nor really cares. From time-to-time people do a double take when seeing the twins together—both men and women. Ryan is very amused.

The first bar that they come to that has two seats open is Fritz' Fish and Grill. Down in the glitzy department but very authentic. The McCallum's order two Cuba Libres and clink glasses.

"I'm really glad you could break away and come down to my playground, Sean says.

"I needed a change of scenery and I want to talk to you."

"This is certainly a change from the world of high finance. Let's just chill and we can talk about heavy stuff later."

"Sounds like a plan. The view is far too interesting."

"Remember what Mom used to say, *don't let your eyes be bigger than your stomach*? Both brothers simultaneously break out in gales of laughter drawing attention to themselves. But who cares? This is South Beach.

Two drinks later, and a lot of bikini clad women strolling along the dock, the entertainment at Fritz' begins in earnest. The band consists of four members, all female impersonators who open with a medley of 70s classics. Ryan is amazed how good the band sounds. The bar gets noisier and nosier and a bit rowdier. Both Ryan and Sean decide to call it a night. Sean has not said a thing about his living circumstances and Ryan decides not to push it. The two make their way to the entrance. Close to fifty people are waiting to get inside. The number of people in the same place at the same time is both exciting and a little creepy. Thoughts of falling and being trampled zip through Ryan's subconscious. He suddenly has a Margaret flashback.

Sean again takes the lead. He is clearly experienced in running the gauntlet in a crowd. Ryan tries to keep up. Suddenly, a man approaches Ryan. He draws a gun from his waistband and shoots Ryan. The noise of the shot is somewhat muffled, but Sean is quite attuned to the sound of gunfire. He quickly backtracks to Ryan who is lying in a pool of blood unresponsive. Sean immediately realizes that the shooter is Carlos Alverez, who mistook Ryan for Sean.

"Shit!" Sean mutters. The sound of a siren brings Sean back to the here and now. He reaches into Ryan's back pocket and removes his wallet and replaces it with his own. He also grabs Ryan's cell phone. Sean crosses himself, touches his brother's forehead and quickly flees the scene.

CHAPTER NINETEEN

The cloudless blue skies quickly give way to thickening black clouds and faint rumbles of thunder. Sean has never been one to panic, but the sight of his dead brother really spooks him. His first reaction is to get as much distance between himself and South Beach as possible. The only silver lining is that Sean's many enemies will now assume he is no longer a problem. Sean's intuitive reaction to swap wallets is now his ticket to freedom. Although he feels remorse, he also feels that a weight has been lifted from his shoulders.

Sean slows his pace, breathes deeply, and decides that he will become Ryan, assume all aspects of his identity, and return to Orlando. Although, he is not sure that he can maintain the charade of being a high finance wizard. He needs a long-term plan. Sean only wishes he had had more time to talk to Ryan. Sean suspected that something has been bothering his brother, but he figured that his *fair-haired* twin's troubles were minor. Sean had been living with trouble forever. Sometimes big trouble.

Knowing that Ryan was extremely methodical, Sean opens Ryan's wallet. Thumbing through the contents,

Sean finds the hotel security card where Ryan was staying, his keyless code for the Mercedes, several charge cards, about $300 in cash, his Florida driver's license, and insurance card. More than enough to assume his new identity. Avoiding the gathering crowds, Sean quickens his gait. He figures the hotel will be a safe haven and give him an opportunity to pull himself together.

"Good evening Mr. McCallum," the doorman chirps. "Looks like we're going to have some showers. You best get inside before it begins."

"Do I need to make reservations in the restaurant?"

"We have a full menu in the bar, which is very informal." Sean senses a slight critical intonation toward his present attire.

"No, I am going up to my room to clean up and dress for dinner. Table for one at 7 would be ideal. Thanks." Sean decides that is how his brother would respond. Sean, on the other hand, might be a bit less polite. This is going to require a lot of adjustments.

Sean also needs to figure out how he can get into his condo and retrieve his laptop, a rather significant stash of cash, bearer bonds, and about forty pounds of gold coins. How fast will the police start investigating? Probably pretty quick considering Sean's reputation. He opts to go up to Ryan's room and change into something less conspicuous, and then walk over to his unit. Although driving would be faster, he is sure the hotel has security cameras in the parking garage. He'll be back in time for his dinner reservation.

Ryan's room is as neat as a pin. Just as Sean had expected. Needless to say, the twins were the same size so the transition from thug to respectable businessman is seamless. Lightweight beige slacks, a solid colour collared shirt and a cashmere sweater casually draped over his shoulders. Loafers with tassels finish the wardrobe. *Voilà.*

Sean elects to be obvious, rather than circumspect.

He exits through the main lobby and engages the desk clerk. "I'll be back in a few minutes. I need to get my briefcase from my car."

"I don't suggest you leave anything of value in your car. Even with our security protocols, theft is still a problem."

"Good point. I'll bring my briefcase back to the room. Thanks."

"You clean up very nicely," the clerk is clearly flirting.

"Will I be admitted to the dining room?"

"Absolutely. Hurry back, it's supposed to start raining any minute."

Sean waves and walks out the main door, knowing his every move is being recorded. He enters the elevator to the garage. It suddenly occurs to him that all he knows is that Ryan drove a Mercedes. No model or color and, of course, the garage is full of Mercedes. Sean pushes the door opening button on the car's remote, hoping that it would honk or flash or something. His luck, as always, holds.

Sean moves to the car, opens the door, and looks in. There is no briefcase on the seats. Maybe Ryan didn't bring a briefcase on vacation. He pushes the trunk release button which pops open with a whooshing sound. A large hunter green canvas briefcase beckons. He quickly empties the contents and slips the strap over his shoulder. It should be able to carry most everything.

He closes the trunk and walks to the elevator. Walking as fast as he can, Sean covers the distance to his condominium building in less than six minutes. He uses the service elevator which he knows is not under surveillance and slips into his unit's back door. He moves through each room with practiced efficiency and retraces his steps, returning to the hotel. Total elapsed time is under twenty minutes. The rain, which held off during his walk, begins in earnest.

Sean returns to the hotel room and places several wrapped bundles of hundred-dollar bills and a couple of bags of coins into the room safe. The bonds are less obvious, so they remain in the briefcase along with the laptop, which he places under the bed.

Sean casually enters the restaurant.

"Table for McCallum," he says.

"Right this way, sir," the maître d responds.

Sean is seated at a table toward the back of the room, which pleases him because he has a view of everything and everyone.

"May I get you a drink?" A very lovely waitperson says in a voice that sounds like she is purring.

"Yes, please. Dry martini, gin martini, with a twist."

"Will you be having dinner?"

"In due course."

"Very good." She turns and walks toward the bar which is quite full.

Happy hour and rain certainly seem to bring folks into the hotel bar. A tuxedo clad piano player sits at a rather garish white grand piano. Thankfully, there is no candelabra in sight. The music is calming. Sean's drink arrives.

"Thank you," he says.

"Anytime, anywhere," she replies. This is the second time since he got to the hotel that a beautiful woman has been suggestive. Maybe the clothes do make the man.

Although Sean feels like gulping down the drink, he slowly sips. He needs to remember that he is Ryan. Sean is dead.

The waitperson returns and asks if he would like another. *Yes*, he answers to himself, "No thank you. I'll probably have a glass of wine with dinner."

"I'll bring you a menu."

"Thank you. Are there any specials tonight?"

"Actually the chef has made a lobster bisque. It's terrific. I had a little before my shift began. The Caesar salad is a perfect complement, with a fresh cheese biscuit."

"Sounds fabulous. Forget the menu. Sign me up. A glass of Chardonnay. Your choice."

"Thank you for your confidence in my taste."

Now, that could lead me to ask, *how do you taste?* But that would be tacky.

The waitperson turns bright red. Smiles, nods, removes the martini glass and . . . winks. This is not the part of South Florida Sean is used to. Maybe I'll go to Palm Beach before I go up to Orlando. I had better get my mind on to the issues at hand. Maybe chilling out for a day will allow me to come up with a plan rather than winging it. Maybe I'll invite the waitperson up to my room after her shift is done. Too many maybes.

The soup arrives with a small decanter.

"I suggest the sherry be added to the soup."

"Sounds good. I thank you for your advice. You seem to have a sense of cuisine."

"I hope to have my own restaurant someday. Small, in a neighborhood where folks work, live, and dine."

"Sounds ideal. Do you have an idea where this paradise might be?"

"Not yet. Please eat before your soup gets cold. Maybe we can talk about it later."

Sean nods. More maybes. "Yes, I would like that."

The soup is indeed terrific. Sean begins to unwind, but not too much to forget who he is and how many people want a piece of him.

CHAPTER TWENTY

Sean can't remember when he slept as soundly. He should be wracked with grief, but all he feels is relief. Maybe his companion for the night had something to do with his sense of euphoria. Maybe it was being given a *do over* button. Ryan would have been pleased with that concept. After a room service breakfast, Doris (that's her name he discovered) announces that she has to leave because she doesn't want to miss class. It turns out that the flirtatious young lady is studying business and culinary arts at the University of Miami. Sean is torn. He would like to continue this relationship, but it poses a plethora of potential problems with his Ryan persona. However, a plan is evolving. Instead of leaving himself open to screwing up everything, he simply says to the powers that be, that he is burned out and is taking some time off to leisurely travel or get a place in the mountains and fish, write, canoe and whatever. Maybe find a little town that needs a restaurant. Once again, too many maybes. Sean is getting ahead of himself.

"Good morning sunshine," Doris whispers. "Time to go. Can we get together later? I'm off tonight and I'd love to show you South Beach."

Now, that's a red flag. "How about a rain check. I mean it. I have to get back to the office today, but I've pretty much made up my mind to take a sabbatical. Then we could try to find your paradise. You've only got a couple more weeks before the semester is over, and I can come down once or twice and then we can hit the open road."

"Are you kidding me just to make me feel better . . . less like a tramp."

"No . . . no . . . absolutely not. I really want to see you again. Soon."

"I believe you and let's just see how this pans out. I suspect it may take you more time to untangle yourself than you think, especially if there is a girl back in Orlando."

Sean's first hurdle. Did his brother have a significant other? He knows about Margaret, so he assumes there is no one else. And besides Ryan lived alone. "There's no one in Orlando or anywhere else for that matter. I'm good. It's mostly business stuff that I have to take care of." Ryan never mentioned any close friends except his old roommate, but he lives up North. As soon as Doris leaves, he had better go through Ryan's phone.

"Let's make a plan," Doris suggests. "I'm off next Tuesday and Wednesday. Why don't we meet somewhere? How about Vero Beach. I can take the train and we can get a room on the ocean and walk along the beach. It will help you unwind."

"You're on. I'll find a place. I will text you my schedule. I'm looking forward to a great new adventure." Sean and Doris embrace.

"Until then." She walks toward the door, turns, blows him a kiss, and leaves.

Sean does not feel relieved as he often did other times he was with a woman all night. He feels kind of empty. Good empty, but empty, nevertheless. The sooner he gets back and wraps up his brother's affairs, the better.

Sean's drive back to Orlando is uneventful, thank goodness. The road from Miami to his office is the scene of accidents, often fatal, on a daily basis. The Mercedes exudes driver confidence, but caution limits Sean to the speed limit and right lane.

He decides to call the office from Ryan's cell, just to give everyone a heads up that he is on his way. His call is answered by a very abrupt receptionist. Sean can't believe Ryan would hire someone so outwardly rude.

"Thank goodness you called. The police in Miami have called several times. I lied and said I was a temp and didn't have your cell number. Then a rather aggressive Detective Polski called and asked, no . . . actually told me, to have you call him the moment I heard from you. Then your attorney called, but he simply said to tell you he called. I'm exhausted."

"I've only been gone two days."

"And then there's the client calls that Margaret usually handles." Sean heard a sniffle from the receptionist.

"I had better make some return calls. Let me pull over and get the numbers for the Miami police and Detective Polski. Hang on."

Sean exits the highway and pulls into a Burger King parking lot. After getting the numbers Sean begins to feel anxious. The Miami police make sense, Detective Polski might be the cop that Ryan talked to, but what does Ryan's attorney want? Suddenly, Sean craves a Whopper and a Coke. Hopefully, that will calm his nerves.

Ryan's cell phone rings. The caller ID says Stephen Blackman—Ryan's lawyer. How can he fool his brother's best friend? Sean answers, "To what do I owe this call?"

"Just a head's up old buddy. I got a call from FBI Agent Dylan, who informed me that your brother was shot last night in South Beach. Apparently you are being followed by the feds hoping to lead them to Sean. They know you two were together. They want to schedule another meeting."

"Shit! Sean dead? Let me get back on the road and I'll call you later."

"Not too much later. You sound funny. Are you okay?"

"Got a cold and just heard my twin was killed. No, I am not okay. I'll call later." Sean hangs up. He hopes he satisfied Attorney Blackman, for at least a little while. Next call he makes is to the Miami police. The extension the receptionist had given Sean is answered immediately.

"Sergeant Tommy Thompson. How may I help you?"

Sean clears his throat before saying, "This is Ryan McCallum, returning your call."

"I've been trying to get in touch with you all morning. Your brother has been shot, and I need to ask you some questions."

"I just heard."

"From whom?"

"My lawyer."

"News travels fast, especially bad news."

"Seems so. I'm on my way to my office right now. Can I call you later this afternoon?"

"I'd rather interview you in person. Are you going to be in Miami again soon?"

"I guess I have to make arrangements. I have to absorb all this."

"I understand. How about day after tomorrow?"

"Let me check and see if my attorney is available. Can't we all Zoom this or something?"

"That's a thought. Let me check from my end. Now that I have your cell number on my caller ID, I will ring you when I know more."

The line goes silent.

So far so good. Stephen can deal with the FBI. Most likely they want to talk to Ryan about the money I have been sending, Sean says to himself. How long can I bluff Stephen? This is getting way too complicated.

There are a lot of things Sean doesn't know about his brother.

The only remaining call is to Detective Polski, whoever he is and whatever he wants. Sean dials.

"Polski . . . may I help you?"

"Detective Polski, this is Ryan McCallum returning your call. How may I help you?"

"First of all, when are you planning on returning from your trip?"

"I don't understand detective. Why should I let you know my specific schedule?" Sean is trying to remain cool, but there is a clear "cop" tone to Detective Polski's voice.

"First of all, I want you to."

"Wait a second Detective. No one ever told me to stay in town. And I don't like your tone."

"In as much as we are investigating a homicide, I don't care about my tone, and I do not like potential witnesses or possibly suspects roaming around without me knowing exactly where they area."

"You have me at a disadvantage detective because I don't know anything more than I already told you." Sean wishes he could remember exactly what Ryan told him.

"The death of Margaret Adams is suspicious, and you are the one under suspicion. By the way, you sound different."

"I have a cold." Sean never realized that he and Ryan didn't sound alike. "What have you found out about her death?"

Sean is on a fishing trip, and he knows it. He just hopes Detective Polski doesn't.

"McCallum, are you still there?" Polski's question brings Sean back into the here and now.

"Yes, Detective. I am listening. What do I have to do with Ms. Adams' death?"

"You mean since you seem to be the last person to see her alive?"

Sean's instinct kicks into high gear.

"The last one except the person responsible for her death, you mean."

"Don't be cute. Just be in my office at 10 AM tomorrow." Polski sounds frustrated. Every good defense requires a good offense.

"I'll check with my attorney and see if he is available and get back to you." Sean presses the END button. Sean wishes he was back in South Beach with Doris. Maybe not such a bad idea. There are too many pieces in play. Sean suddenly feels a tightening in his chest.

CHAPTER TWENTY-ONE

Sean pulls the Mercedes into the first gas station he can. He parks as far away from the pumps as possible. His bravado façade is beginning to crack. He could always handle any confrontation he had with cops, but these were confrontations created by Ryan, of which he has very little knowledge. Breathe deeply. It's time for a game plan.

The Miami sergeant is simple. He had just left the scene after having a couple of drinks with his brother, the deceased, and doesn't know anything. He can't deny having been with him since they were seen together. As Ryan he can honestly say he doesn't know much about whatever business his brother was in. He seldom saw him, and they spoke only rarely. Ryan's phone records will substantiate the story.

The FBI is a little sketchier and quite frankly, more frightening. He had always avoided the feds. They were relentless once they get started and have infinite resources at their disposal. Many of the people he knew who got tangled up with the feds ended up in jail, or even worse. Attorney Blackman seems unfazed by the FBI's inquiries.

Sean's gut tells him to go with the flow. The entire investigation probably relates to his investments with Ryan. No big deal. The paper trail is perfect. But he had better find out . . . tomorrow.

This thing with Margaret is something altogether different. Sean senses that his brother is being fingered for her death. Certainly being at Margaret's doesn't help, but there's no motive.

Too many irons in the fire. Should he deal with them one at a time or try to get hold of the money Ryan was investing for him and disappear? If he grabs the money, his cover is blown. Plan B: get as many of Ryan's liquid assets as possible and enter the deep and dark world of fugitives. If Sean's money remains invested with Ryan's firm, then the twin exchange is somewhat more secure. Is it?

Sean feels the sweat rolling down his back under the nicely laundered shirt with the initial RM embroidered on the cuff. For the next few days, he has to pretend that he has a wicked bad case of the flu. Communicate by text or email. If the phone rings ignore it if practical, otherwise cough and sneeze as much as possible. Schedule the cops in Miami for Friday. That gives him three days to deal with the FBI and the homicide detective. Start now.

The email to the Miami police is short and sweet.

> *I can be in Miami on Friday afternoon to meet with you at your office. Please confirm. Ryan McCallum*

Next, he texts Ryan's attorney. Does he call him Steve, Stephen, or some nickname? Skip the introduction.

> *You caught me a little off guard with news about Sean. How does this affect me? My head cold may be flu. I feel terrible and I ache all over.*

Going home to sleep. If it is something you can handle, please do. I have had all my vaccines, but I will probably get a COVID test anyway. I don't have time to quarantine myself. Thanks.

Detective Polski will have to wait. Get home and go on the computer to see if there are any articles about Margaret's death. Stream a couple of local news casts.

The constriction in Sean's chest eases. A plan is always the best medicine. Since Margaret isn't at the office to whom should he send an email explaining his continuing absence. By Irish good luck or a stroke of genius, Sean opens Ryan's wallet and finds the answer. On his business card is the email address of his assistant, Nanci, with an "i." He quickly types a short note, emphasizing that he may have to self-quarantine if he tests positive for COVID, but that he will check email and text regularly, when not sleeping, of course.

Since he just left Doris, she can wait until he settles into a "Ryan routine". Suddenly, the sun is shining . . . or has he simply not noticed. Although Sean has never been to Ryan's condominium, he knows the address and has driven by on several occasions, unbeknownst to his brother.

Sean is pleasantly pleased with the Mercedes. He has always driven far less opulent cars. In his line of work, keeping a low profile is very important. He still has no idea how he is going to transition into Ryan's persona, but he just bought a couple of days to develop a strategy. Sean briefly considers calling a close friend and asking him to check up on Detective Polski but rejects the idea immediately. Way too dangerous. He can deal with the cops once he finishes his own research.

Ryan's condo is rather 'different' than Sean had expected. There is no evidence of high-tech gadgetry associated with wealthy, single high rolling financial types. Everything is low key. Sean has to laugh at the simplicity of his brother's lifestyle.

Mom taught us the value of money conservation, he thought.

Ryan's laptop is still in the trunk of the car. Once inside, he powers up both his and Ryan's computers. Fortunately, his brother was as nostalgic as he is. They both used the same password, 1218@home—the address of the McCallum's house. Sean is a little uncomfortable reading his brother's emails, but he needs to get up to speed as quickly as possible. There is little revealing or suggestive about the emails on the computer except a missive from Ryan's lawyer/friend.

> Get well. COVID is nothing to screw around with. The feds want to know if you know anything about Sean's will. They seem to know or at least speculate that Sean sent you money to invest and they want confirmation. I played dumb. They have a problem. Inasmuch as Sean had not been charged with any crime, they can't get to his money, and they can't charge a dead man with a crime. They have no subpoena power to get information. No investigation, no need to cooperate. Dead end so to speak. If Sean did give you money to invest and if he did have a Will and made you beneficiary or died intestate without other heirs, the money, if he gave you any, it's yours. The feds are pissed, but they can't do anything. We will talk when you recover. Stephen

One problem down, two to go. All he has to do is probate Sean's estate like any brother would do and the dough is his. Pretty slick. Sean wants to keep the Miami cops on their heels, so he emails the investigating officer and tells him that Friday is a *'maybe'* pending the outcome of a COVID test and he will let him know as soon as he gets the result.

Two down, one to go.

Sean decides that he should try and find out as much as possible about Margaret, especially the details of her death. He assumes there is a news report he can stream. Maybe there is some correspondence between his twin and Margaret that will give him more insight into their relationship. Polski is still the wild card. He needs to know what Polski knows. A hot shower and a Scotch on ice will make the process seem less onerous.

CHAPTER TWENTY-TWO

S ean starts to squirm in his chair. 'How can people sit in front of a computer for hours a day?' he asks himself, although he has to admit he is better informed now than he was a short time ago. He knows, for instance, that Stan Polski is a third generation Orlando cop and had been a rising star in the department. He handles mostly nontraditional homicides—those that are not shoot 'em ups where the victim and the shooter have been identified. His specialty is the more sophisticated and hence more complicated cases. Sean reads an early article where the victim had died of an apparent heart attack, but in fact had been administered a lethal dose of digitalis, which gives the same indicia. Sean assumes that the department considers Margaret's death to be sophisticated and complicated although Sean doesn't see it that way. It smells like Polski is making a mountain out of a mole hill.

He also gleans from the articles that Polski is relentless in his pursuit of the bad guy. Not a good sign. However, the esteemed detective seems to have stepped on a lot of toes. Sean muses that his brother is in more trouble than Sean. Maybe his swapping of identities wasn't the best idea he ever had. Then again, if he can get both his money and Ryan's money, then he can live in comfort off the grid quite well for a long time. Sean sips his drink. He needs a clear head.

The major problem he sees is how to handle the pit bull cop with an attitude. He can play hard ball and make him prove his case: motive, means, and opportunity. Since Ryan was admittedly at the scene, opportunity is no-brainer. Motive—why would he kill his best friend? Even acknowledging they were having an argument, certainly that doesn't rise to a motive for murder. Means? The news reports were very vague about the cause of Margaret's death, only that it occurred by her pool. If he is correct that the cops performed an autopsy, then the fact that she didn't die from drowning certainly makes Ryan more suspect since people seldom fall into their own pools after they are dead.

Sean takes another sip. What if Margaret wasn't dead from the fall as Ryan in his near frantic condition thought she was, and he pushed her into the pool while she was alive? Not good. The autopsy results are crucial. There are too many unknowns. Sean is again feeling that the identity switch is substantially more problematic than he initially thought.

Another epiphany. If Sean is arrested as Ryan and the cops run his fingerprints through the system, everything goes to hell in a hand basket. There really wouldn't be a reason to search the fingerprint database since the cops are arresting a person they have already identified. Sloppy, very sloppy.

The light is failing outside, and Sean is surprised that it is already a little past seven. Perfect! He dials Polski's office, assuming the good detective is gone for the day.

"Polski, here."

Sean stutters in response and fakes a cough. "Sorry, I think I have the flu. This is Ryan McCallum, and I am not going to be able to meet you tomorrow. My attorney is in the middle of a trial in Boston and won't be able to get away until the middle of next week. He said to tell you he can get a protective order from the judge if he needs to. Also, I am going to my doctor in the morning for a COVID test. He told me the results take about 48 hours and that I should self-quarantine as a precaution. On a more practical note, I don't know any more than I did the other day when we spoke, which call you may recollect, was initiated by me."

"Are you through?" Polski asks. Without waiting for a reply he says, "I really don't care about your lawyer's schedule. There are plenty of attorneys here in Orlando."

"Stop right there Detective Polski. I may not be a lawyer, but I know about intimidation. I am more than willing to tell Attorney Blackman to tell the nice judge in Boston that a homicide dick in Florida is harassing his client for no good reason. If you have sufficient cause, arrest me. Don't try the 'come in for questioning' routine. I came forward and said my peace. I signed your summary of our conversation. I have been cooperative and as helpful as the information I possess permits." Sean starts to cough for effect. "Now, have a good evening. I am going to try to get some sleep and feel better."

Sean hangs up the phone. A smile creeps across his face. *Nice job, hot shot.* He takes another sip of scotch and decides to call Doris, using the fake flu as an excuse to make the conversation short. He dials.

"Hi, this is Doris. You've reached my voice mail. Please leave a message and I'll get back to you as soon as possible."

"Hey kid, this is Ryan." Fake cough. "Got myself a cold or something. Going to bed . . . alone. Call in the morning." Sean's emotional barometer is all over the place. Does he feel sadness that he can't reach Doris or anger? Or jealousy? As is Sean's nature, the conflict is quickly resolves itself by the ringing of his phone. He hesitates. How did Ryan answer? Was he formal or informal? Just answer and say 'hello.'

"Hello?"

"I'm sorry I missed your call. I was in the shower." Doris' voice purrs.

"I am sorry I missed your shower." That was the best line Sean could come up with.

"Raincheck?" Doris sounds better and better.

"You bet."

"When?"

"That's a bit more complicated. I started to feel a cold coming on and now I feel lousy. I am having a COVID test tomorrow. I suggest you do the same. South Beach is not exactly a germ-free environment."

"I feel fine, but it's better to be safe. I wear a mask when I am in crowds except at work. The boss doesn't like us to wear masks. He says it frightens tourists. If I test positive, I bet I got COVID from someone right off an airplane or a cruise ship. But I have had all my shots."

Sean realizes that he has been a bit negligent in the booster follow-up department.

"I'm sure it's nothing, but better get ahead of the curve. My doctor has advised me to stay at home until he gets the results. So, depending on whether I test negative or not controls my immediate travel plans."

"I understand. Just let me know what the doctor says. Your health is important . . . to me."

Sean can't believe he has only known this girl for 24 hours.

"Thanks darling. I will check in tomorrow after my test."

"Ironic. I have an exam tomorrow also."

"Huh?"

"The course is called Culinary Economics, but I have a pretty good handle on the material." Doris chuckles.

"You are unbelievable. Love you kiddo." Sean hangs up, not waiting for a reply from Doris.

Sean is rather pleased with himself. He put out all the fires, both his and Ryan's. Down deep inside, Sean's stomach rumbles, reminding him that he hasn't eaten since early morning.

Ryan's refrigerator is a barren wasteland of expired labels and slightly over ripe fruit and vegetables. Is this how the other half lives? Sean decides that he shouldn't really be surprised, his brother probably eats out every night, which is totally out of the question.

More likely than not, both the Orlando PD and the feds are watching the condo and a nighttime sortie would be noted.

Reluctantly, Sean returns to the refrigerator. The milk doesn't smell awful and the date on the egg carton still has a few days before expiration. A package of English muffins in the freezer looks very appealing. It won't be the first time Sean has had scrambled eggs and muffins for dinner.

CHAPTER TWENTY-THREE

Sleep comes quickly to Sean. He didn't realize how totally exhausted he is. Eight hours in dreamland is surprisingly restful. Although he's no closer to resolving Ryan's problems, he feels that the 'old Sean' is pretty much free and clear. Even his enemies, of which there are many, can't kill him twice. Funeral arrangements will have to be arranged, but until the Miami PD release the body, there is nothing to be done. He'll have to retain an attorney in South Florida to handle the probate of Sean's estate, which other than the condo in South Beach and a few thousand dollars in a checking account are all 'offshore' holdings which have listed Ryan as POD (payable on death) beneficiary. The condo in Grand Cayman may take a while to unwind but since Sean's Will is very specific; his twin gets everything. Fortunately, the original Will is currently in the green canvas brief case he used to gather everything from his apartment before his hasty departure. Simple is always the best resolution. Since Sean had appointed Ryan as executor, it is logical for the Will to be in Ryan's files. Perfect. When he gets an attorney, give him the Will. End of subject.

In order to keep up his COVID ruse, Sean decides to call Ryan's doctor for an appointment. Once again, his very organized brother makes it easy. Scrolling through Ryan's phone contact list he finds the name of his PCP, Dr. Sidney Helman.

"Hello, this is Ryan McCallum, cough, cough. I am a patient of the office and am feeling rather poorly. In an abundance of caution, I thought I should get a COVID test."

Sean patiently awaits a reply.

"Mr. McCallum," a young female voice responds. "I am sorry you are not feeling well. Do you have a fever or chills or aches?"

"None of the above, but I am tired and am coughing and sneezing a lot."

"That's actually a good sign. We are recommending that our patients do not get tested unless they experience certain symptoms including breathing difficulty, elevated temperature, and other traditional flu-like responses. We are suggesting at least 48 hours of basic bed rest. It sounds like you have a basic cold, but please monitor yourself. If there are any changes, call us immediately. Your chart indicates that the only meds you take are over the counter vitamins, which we suggest you continue. Are you okay with that?"

"Can I get a note from the doctor to give to my employer?" Sean laughs.

"That can be arranged except your chart lists you as a partner in your firm, so to whom should the excuse be written." The nurse giggles.

"Touché. Thanks for your advice. I could use a few days rest anyway. I'll let you know if I experience any changes, including getting better. Bye now." Sean hangs up.

His excuse is now firmly established. Next item of the agenda is food. Sean decides to search the internet for a grocery delivery service and place an order for three days. With meticulous care, Sean plans meals and a list of ingredients required. He does a quick search of his brother's pantry which he concludes is very sparse indeed. After making the necessary arrangements, using Ryan's credit card, Sean decides that he should shower and shave and try to scrounge a cup of coffee. Since Sean is convinced that he is being watched by Polski and/or the FBI, the food delivery service will add further credibility to his saga of sickness.

Sean doubts that his phone, actually Ryan's, or the computer are being monitored. It would probably take a Court order and as the lawyers say, 'there is no probable cause'.

Sean's idea to buy a place in Grand Cayman was largely because the islands are so beautiful. Being protective of banking activities is a definite plus. Financial crimes are hardly considered crimes at all. However, Margaret's death might upset the apple cart. Even the most secretive countries frown upon crimes of violence and bend over backwards to rid themselves of the bad guys. Extradition for murder would be automatic.

Since the Grand Caymans do not require a visa for an American staying less than six months, Sean feels he should carefully examine that option in detail. The first thing he has to do is find Ryan's passport. Once the probate is completed and Ryan (Sean) becomes the owner of real estate, he will be eligible for residency status. If he was still

Sean, this would be a no brainer, but the Margaret thing has him spooked. If Polski doesn't have any other leads, which he won't because there are none, guess who becomes the number one, and only, suspect? It is unlikely that the homicide detective will chalk up Margaret's death to an accident. He is just not the type until he has exhausted every other option leaving Ryan McCallum flapping in the breeze. A sense of loneliness overwhelms Sean. He is used to handling things on his own terms, but this is a bit much. Maybe he should try and find a local criminal attorney and not depend upon Stephen. Sounds like a plan. But who? Asking former colleagues for a referral is out of the question.

Shower, shave, and coffee and then start looking for a legal pit bull, which can't be that hard . . . can it? Interviewing lawyers is about the last thing that Sean wants to do. Focus is required and right now his head is spinning. What about searching big murder cases that he has heard about where the defendant got off. That's the lawyer he wants. However, none comes to mind. What he really needs is a fixer who can prevent the case from going any further. Winning at trial, albeit better than losing, is still not a great result, especially because it will take years to resolve and all he wants right now is to lie on the beach in the Cayman Islands, preferably with Doris.

The process of lawyer shopping goes more quickly than anticipated. Orlando doesn't have that many top-notch criminal lawyers. They have a zillion car crash ambulance chasers, whose names are splashed all over the television-day and night, but the criminal bar is small and usually low key. After about an hour making calls, Sean, as Ryan, has set up four very promising meetings for tomorrow and one conference call for later today.

After re-reading Polski's summary of Ryan's call, Sean decides that he should stick to the account verbatim. No elaborations. No recently recalled memory. Keep it simple. He went to Margaret's at her request. They each had a glass of wine. They had a disagreement and Ryan left. That's it. No, he didn't see someone lurking in the bushes. No, he did not see another car pull into Margaret's driveway. And no, neither he nor anyone he knew had any reason to do her harm. That's it.

The next order of business is to search for Ryan's passport. Where to begin is more difficult than it might seem in a relatively compact condominium. Bookshelves line several walls. Sean has to think like Ryan and not like himself. Sean chuckles at the thought that he would probably put the passport in a hollowed-out book for safe keeping, but Ryan didn't have a need for safe keeping. Sean concludes that it is in plain sight. Hurrying to the bedroom, Sean opens the nightstand drawer. Low and behold. He finds the passport and a paper upon which is written the location of Ryan's Will, his life insurance policies, his birth certificate, and his baptismal certificate. His brother was so disgustingly organized. Sean has to grin at his brother's predictable habits. He basically does the same thing, except that he always keeps his passport with him at all times.

Looking at Ryan's passport photo, it suddenly strikes him. Ryan parted his hair from left to right, while Sean parts his hair from right to left. Sean quickly returns to the bathroom and stares at his hair. He tries to comb it to look like Ryan but it looks funny since it had been cut differently. Until he can get to a barbershop, he'll wear a baseball cap in public. That simply will not work interviewing lawyer's representing yourself as a successful captain of the financial world. Try parting in the middle as a compromise. His new look until he gets it cut properly. He also remembers that Ryan is right-handed, and he is left. He needs to practice signing Ryan's name. So much to do, so little time. Better than the alternative.

CHAPTER TWENTY-FOUR

Sean is aware that his sick-call sabbatical will shortly come to an end. His video call with lawyer #1 did not give him a warm and fuzzy feeling. The lawyer was too slick, too full of himself. He needs a bulldog who is well-known and respected in the legal community. Someone who Detective Polski isn't going to screw with. Someone with connections. Sean hopes that his meetings tomorrow are more productive. He needs to be in the role of an indignant model citizen who is being harassed by a headline grabbing cop. Time to chill.

Sean is pleased that he has decided to call Donna. She is a breath of fresh air which he badly needs.

"Hey honey, how was your day?"

"It was really busy. I am working on my term paper, which is actually an investment summary with a detailed business plan, and it is going more slowly than I had hoped. Also, the season seems to be longer this year. A lot of guests at the hotel," Doris responds.

"I can take a look at it if you'd like. I have a little experience with start-ups. Maybe I can be an investor, or we can make it a joint venture. How does the Cayman Islands sound?"

"You're teasing me, aren't you?"

"No, I'm not. I have a place I just inherited in Grand Cayman and the island is booming with high rollers . . . all of whom not only appreciate great food, but can afford it. And I need to get away from this rat race."

"I'm out of school in a little more than two weeks. How does that sound?"

Doris sounds excited, which makes Sean . . . excited.

"Do you have a passport?"

"No, mine expired years ago and I never had the need to renew it."

"Then my dear, I want you to go down to the post office and apply, right away. Bring your old passport if you have it. Renewal is faster than a new application. I hope to be down to see you early next week. I want to take you shopping for a new island wardrobe."

"That's sounds, like, so terrific. I hate wearing the same old uniform every day and night."

"I need to make sure the condo is ready for us. Let's plan to go on the 24th, that's four weeks from today. I think we should get an open-ended return flight. No rush to get back . . . if ever."

"Ryan, you are a dream come true. I can't even fathom that all I have worked toward might actually come true."

"Not might come true, but will come true. Count on it sweetie. Count on it." Sean exudes confidence, as Ryan, of course.

"I've got to get through the next two weeks and this dumb paper, and then paradise here we come." Doris is out of breath excited.

"I've got a couple of important meetings tomorrow, so I won't be able to call until later in the evening. Okay?"

"Perfect . . . Ryan . . . you're the greatest." They discontinue the call.

Sean suddenly decides that he is starving. The mention of starting a restaurant in Grand Cayman has real appeal. If he could get that stupid cop to accept that he's got nothing to go on, As they say in the song, things are looking up. Chinese take-out delivered. That's the answer. Well, one of the answers.

When Sean wakes up the next morning he is starving.

"I guess Chinese food doesn't stick to your ribs," he mutters.

After a cup of coffee, two would give him the jitters, he searches Ryan's closet for the appropriate suit to wear to his interviews. He decides on a dark blue, light weight power suit. Custom made no doubt. White shirt, regimental tie and a pocket silk and Ryan is reincarnated.

Assuming that an initial interview with a lawyer will be no longer than an hour, Sean has given himself plenty of time between appointments. Orlando has a fairly compact downtown, so Sean elects to Uber to his first appointment and then walk to the others.

Neil Blakely's credentials seem perfect for a case like this. Florida native, West Point, George Washington Law School, twelve years active duty as a Judge Advocate prosecutor of high-profile cases and now a defense attorney with a very impressive record of acquittals, but even more important, an impressive record of pre-trial resolutions. He is well respected by both the bench and the bar. Cops tend to avoid bringing cases to the State Attorney when they know Blakely represents the accused. At 6' 4", retired Major

Blakely, is an imposing figure. Not cheap, but Sean only wants results, and as quickly as possible. The sooner he is gone, the better.

The lobby of Blakely and Associates is understated, functional and without any of the trappings usually associated with high powered law firms. Quite refreshing Sean thinks. At least his money isn't going to be spent on frivolousness.

"Mr. McCallum, Mr. Blakely will see you now," the very matronly receptionist announces. No frivolousness. Sean glances at his watch, 9:02. Right on time. A very good sign.

"Good morning, Mr. McCallum, how can I help you?" Attorney Blakely has a surprisingly high voice for such a large man.

"Please call me Ryan. I have an extremely pushy police detective trying to connect me to the death of my very close friend and business colleague, Margaret Adams. I want him off my back. I have been totally cooperative, but he is trying to bully me."

Attorney Blakely holds up his hand. "I need you to tell me everything . . . from the top. If you have no objections, I'd like to record your comments. It allows me to concentrate on what you are saying without having to write down what you are telling me.

Since this is client-attorney conversation, anything you say is privileged. I need you to tell me everything, regardless of what you think might be the implication. I hate surprises, so I need the entire story from the beginning."

"Fair enough. Let me start by saying that when I learned of Margaret's death from the television, I called Detective Polski, he's the lead investigator, and told him what I am about to tell you. I later signed a statement to that effect." Sean hands Attorney Blakely a copy of the police statement.

He reads it quickly once and then again more slowly a second time.

"The only thing not included is the reason Margaret and I were arguing that night. He didn't ask and I didn't volunteer. I have reviewed the entire episode a hundred times and what I said then and what I can repeat to you is exactly the same. I loved Margaret. We'd been close for several years although we never discussed living together or marriage. It wasn't either of our respective styles, having each been burned once."

"What did you argue about?" Attorney Blakely quietly asks.

"My brother. My identical twin brother, Sean. Apparently, he was under investigation by the FBI, and they interviewed me in the presence of my civil attorney, Stephen Blackman of Boston. We were roommates in college, and he has represented me before regarding an SEC investigation. In neither instance was I the target.

My brother had been sending me money to invest for some time, and Margaret wanted me to tell the FBI. I told her that they didn't ask, and on advice of counsel, I didn't volunteer. Margaret didn't like Sean, although she never met him. She thought he was a low life crook. I told her it was none of her business. That's why we argued. Since I knew that I wasn't going to change her mind, I left her house. She was alive, albeit pretty angry with me. That's it. There was no reason why I would want to harm her, much less kill her. I figured it would blow over. The feds would get Sean, or they wouldn't. It was not my fight."

"And that's it?"

"That's it. Polski is trying to make me look like a murderer. He has nothing to go on because there is nothing there. What reason would I have to hurt Margaret? What motive? Since he has no other suspects, he is making me his entire case."

"Cops are often like that. They go crazy if the pieces don't fit together nice and neat. Are you absolutely sure you didn't leave anything out?"

"Positively. The irony is that Sean was killed several days ago in South Florida. Completely unrelated to this matter, I assure you. So it hasn't been a great week."

"Wow. That's a lot coming at you at one time."

"Yup. That's why I want to get this behind me and run off to the islands for a while."

"Understood. Well, here's the game plan. First, I want you to review and sign a fee agreement. The retainer will be $10,000. Next, I will contact Detective Polski and try to figure out where he is coming from. Hopefully, I can get access to his investigation file. See what he has or thinks he has. Then we will meet again. Your case appears to be an all or nothing matter. Either the cops have enough to go to the prosecutor's office or they don't. If they think they have a case, better to know now. Make them go to a Grand Jury and see if they can get an indictment. If Polski is trying to crack you because he has some kind of cop instinct, but no facts except circumstantial tidbits, all of which you have admitted to, I will go to the State Attorney's myself and tell him that this is bull shit and his office's resources are better spent on something real. Let them say that there was foul play, and you were the player. If not . . . drop it."

Sean likes the way Blakely gets to the point. He feels he has made a wise choice in selecting counsel. However, as with everything, the proof is in the pudding.

"Shall I give you a check now?" Sean asks.

"I'll have my secretary send over the fee agreement by e-mail. You can read it and sign it electronically if it is acceptable, and e-mail it back. You can use PayPal to send the funds. I've got a busy afternoon, so I won't be able to reach out to Detective Polski until tomorrow in any event. Hopefully we can reach a speedy and successful conclusion."

"I certainly hope so. Between you and me, I am getting tired of the rat race. I need to go to Miami to settle my brother's affairs and then I need a long vacation, preferably somewhere with no phone service." Sean smiles. "Definitely no phone service."

"Sounds like a plan. Hope I can get you on your way. I should know a lot more tomorrow after chatting with Detective Polski. If he want's to play hard ball, I will reach out to the prosecutor's office." Attorney Blakely exudes confidence.

"Thanks. I won't take up any more of your time." Sean rises, shakes Blakely's hand, and leaves.

Although lawyers are not high on Sean's list of favorite people, he feels confident that Neil Blakely is the exception. The first order of business is to cancel his other appointments, have a bagel with cream cheese and figure out how to liquidate his money, as well as Ryan's, and safely transfer funds to his bank in Grand Cayman. Since he has Ryan's passport, maybe he should take a quick trip after tidying up things in South Florida. As Ryan, he needs to call the office and tell them to close Sean's account. Since the account lists Ryan as the beneficiary of the payable on death option, the firm should be able to cut him a check. They'll probably want a death certificate. That means Miami. Suddenly, a thought occurs to Sean. Why not simply close the account and have the funds deposited into Sean's account in Grand Cayman. Later he can withdraw the money and put it into a new account in Ryan's name. Perfect.

CHAPTER TWENTY-FIVE

Sean begins to doubt himself, which is not something that makes him feel comfortable. Too many pieces are fitting together. He has always experienced loose ends. Maybe everything is going to be different as Ryan. Luck of the Irish. Sean opens Ryan's cell and speed dials Nanci.

"Mr. McCallum's office, how may I help you?"

"Nanci, it's me, although I don't feel like me." Sean coughs. "Is there anything that needs my immediate attention?"

"No, everything is pretty much under control."

"Pretty much?" Sean coughs again.

"Mrs. Gallini insists on talking to you and you alone. Something about her great Uncle Carlos. She is very adamant."

"Can you text me her phone number. I will call her as soon as I get up the energy. I should charge her by the hour. She can talk the brass ear off a tin Monkey." Sean chuckles.

"I haven't heard that expression in years. My grandmother used it a lot, especially about newscasters."

"At least she could switch channels," Sean chuckles again. "Oh, Nanci, I heard from my brother Sean, and he's decided to close his account at the firm, about which I am not unhappy. He wants the funds transferred into his account in Grand Cayman. As soon as I get the routing number and account number, I'll email you."

"Shouldn't we get something for the file signed by him authorizing the transfer?"

This is a detail Sean hadn't thought through. "The account is set up for electronic instructions so when I get the account information, I will make sure he authorizes the transfer and e-signs. It will suffice because we have his computer's IP address from when the account was initially opened. The sooner the money is transferred, the better. The firm will be able to isolate itself from those meddling people I met with the other day from the FBI. Good riddance, I say."

"Sounds good, sir, I will get the necessary forms to close the account and attach the e-authorization and move the funds to his offshore account."

"Thanks." More coughing. "I think I've talked too much. Just send me Mrs. G's number. Bye." Sean immediately ends the call.

Who the hell is Mrs. Gallini and what does she want? Maybe he should email her and tell her he is 'deathly' ill and will get back to her when he feels better. With his luck, she'd come over to the condo with a container of freshly made minestrone. Nothing to do except wait a little before sending the Grand Cayman banking information to the office. They say that curiosity killed the cat, but Sean has always taken the position that curiosity is the source of all knowledge and the knowledge he was curious about is his brother's assets. If he is going to take a sabbatical, then he had better be able to access to Ryan's wealth such as it is. Sean assumes his twin's persona and methodically searches the entire condominium. He even looks for a hidden safe to no avail. Ryan must have kept his papers at the office. That may pose a problem. He speed dials the office.

"Nanci, it's me again. It looks like I am going to have to stay away from people for several days. The doctor does not think I have COVID, but that I have some kind of regular type virus if there is such a thing." Sean fake coughs. "I think I should come into the office after hours and go through my mail. There are several personal asset statements my accountant wants. I have no idea why. Could you put all my statements for the last ninety days into a folder on my desk and I'll pick them up."

"Why don't I make copies and have a courier service deliver them to you."

"Great idea. Include everything I should be looking at and I'll reply by email. You're a life saver. Thanks." Another cough. "I promise to call Mrs. G later this afternoon. And I owe you my brother's banking info. Thanks." Sean quickly disconnects the calls.

This is working out better than he thought. Searching Ryan's office when he had never been there before could be a big problem, which Nanci has now resolved. When should he plan on heading to the Islands? Give his attorney two weeks, max. Either everything is resolved, or it is unlikely to have an imminent conclusion. In order to get him back from Grand Cayman, the cops would have to charge him with murder and a grand jury indite him. Unlikely. One thing at a time. Marshall all the assets under Ryan's name and place them into an offshore account where they will be safe and sound. Next, Sean decides he has to email the condominium resort superintendent in Grand Cayman to make sure his unit is ready to occupy. He also has to reach out to the garage that stores his car. Sean feels a pang of indecision—Doris. Does he trust his heart which says, 'go for it' or his head which says, 'get settled and then decide'?

The best thing to do when you've got a million things on your mind is to take a nap, however Sean, as Ryan, better call Mrs. Gallini. He dials.

"Hello?" A heavily accented woman answers the call.

"This is Ryan McCallum. I'm sorry I haven't gotten back to you, but I was out of town for a couple of days and when I got back I had the worst cold. How can I help you, Ma'am?"

"It's my son, Peter's, wife. I have always thought she was after him for his money and now I'm sure of it."

"How are you sure of it?" Sean hopes this conversation is not going to become a soap opera.

"She wants him to buy a new house. Can you imagine. They have a perfectly nice house right next door to me."

"How long have they been married?"

"Don't you remember? You were at the wedding. It'll be seven years in September. And they haven't given me any grandchildren."

"I think I understand. Would you like me to do something in particular?"

"Yes, I want you to talk some sense into him. My Peter is being led to the poor house by this woman." Mrs. G's voice has risen several octaves.

"Have you talked to Peter or more importantly, his wife?"

"Of course not. That's your job."

"Let me look at his portfolio. If I can find a financial reason not to buy a house, I will talk with him, otherwise I don't think it is my place to tell him what to do."

"I suppose you're right. If only his father was still alive. Thank you Mr. McCallum for listening to a worried old lady."

"You are just being a concerned mother. I will review his portfolio and reach out to him if appropriate. Goodbye, Mrs. Gallini." Sean disconnects.

'Did Ryan have to deal with this shit on a daily basis? I'd go crazy,' Sean mutters to himself.

Sean's 'to do' list is getting shorter by the minute. He decides that he had better call the Miami police before they think he is ducking them. He dials.

"Sergeant Tommy Thompson."

"Sergeant, This is Ryan McCallum." Cough. "I just wanted to check in."

"You still sound terrible, Mr. McCallum. The good news is that you don't need to come down here in any hurry. We have identified and arrested the shooter, Carlos Alverez."

"Name doesn't ring a bell," Sean responds.

"Apparently, Señor Alverez knew your brother quite well. Rumor on the street is that your brother, Sean, was seen hanging around Señora Alverez while the husband was in jail. Apparently, the husband was quite jealous and decided to shoot your brother. However, it seems that your brother did not have a relationship with the wife. We interviewed her and quite a few other folks and although your brother ran into the damsel at a diner and asked her to join him. They left separately. Next, they met at an anniversary party for some mutual acquaintances. Again, they left separately. That's it. So Carlos got it wrong, and Sean got a bullet. Case closed. The DA is looking at murder one and maybe the death sentence. So, unless you have something to add, we are closing the file and letting the prosecutor's office handle it."

"Wow! Talk about being in the wrong place at the wrong time." Sean takes a deep breath to take in the fact that Ryan was killed for nothing. "Thanks Sergeant. I need to process this."

"I understand. Goodbye." The line goes silent.

Sean can feel himself losing it. He can't decide whether he should scream, swear, throw something or cry. He chooses the latter.

CHAPTER TWENTY-SIX

It is definitely too early in the day to start drinking. Sean does not have the luxury of feeling sorry for himself or for Ryan. He doesn't have the time to feel, period. The downstairs buzzer snaps Sean into the here and now.

'Who the hell could that be?' Sean asks himself.

"Hello?" Sean answers the buzz through the security speaker.

"I'm here from the office, sir. Nanci said I was to deliver files to you."

Sean sighs in relief. "I'll be right down. Thanks."

Sean looks at himself in the mirror. Unless the messenger worked with Ryan closely, he'd never spot the difference. Just to be sure, Sean dons a surgical mask. He wanted his encounter to get back to the office to satisfy curiosity. He unlocks the unit door, shutting it behind him and places his security pass against the screen at the elevator. The panel beeped in recognition of his identification. 'Fooled the damn machine,' Sean muttered as the doors open. Entering the cage he firmly pushes the button for the lobby.

The messenger is a twenty-something kid who was obviously trying to get his foot in the door of the firm, even if it meant starting at the bottom. Good for him.

"Mr. McCallum?" The young man asked.

"Although a shadow of myself with this damn flu, it is I. Let me show you my license so you can report that you checked my ID. It will make you look efficient."

"Thank you, sir, although you look identical to your picture hanging in the office lobby." The messenger offers a package to Sean.

"Just put it down. I am not sure if I am contagious. And thanks for rushing over here."

The young man does as requested, nods, and retreats out the building door. Sean steps forward and retrieves the package.

"Now, that went well. Within a half-hour everyone will know that Ryan is alive and well, albeit suffering from the flu," Sean says to no one in particular.

He retraces his steps and re-enters the condo. Placing the file on the dining room table, he decides that it really isn't too early for a drink after all. A small one.

The material Nanci sent over is voluminous. Either Ryan is a very rich man, or he needs to clean up his spam mail. The notification tone on Ryan's computer says that a message has arrived. It beeps a second time. Sean opens the laptop and sees an email from Attorney Blakely's office and one from Nanci. He opens the lawyer missive first. The engagement letter and fee agreement, as expected. The email from Nanci is a reminder to send her the routing and account numbers for the Grand Cayman account.

Deciding to kill two birds with one stone, proverbially speaking of course, Sean opens his laptop and begins to compose an email to Nanci.

Ryan asked that I email you directly since he is running out of gas. My account number in the Grand Cayman is 19460812 and the routing number is 3519121824. I hereby authorize you to transfer my funds at Simpson, Tucker, and Co. to the afore-mentioned account and I hereby hold harmless Simpson, Tucker, and Co. from any claims that may be made as a result of said transfer. Ryan told me that my IP address should be sufficient verification of my authorization, but if you need anything else, please feel free to contact me directly at this email address. Thank you. Sean McCallum

Based on Nanci's obvious efficiency, the transfer should hit his account tomorrow.

Sean starts to read the email from the attorney's office but after about two pages of legal gobbledygook, he e-signs the document and sends it back with a note that he will transfer money electronically upon receipt of the firm's deposit information. His slate is clear. Now, comes the hard part—waiting. Maybe there's an old Humphrey Bogart movie on one of the cable channels. It's time to have that drink. Smiling to himself, he thinks, *Maybe Ingrid Bergman will walk into his gin joint.* "Sounds like a plan," Sean mutters.

Well, it's a plan until Attorney Blakely gets back to him. He has got to get that damn detective Polski off his back.

Sean's day turns into evening and then night. He wants to call Doris, but he is not sure what he wants to say. So, he defers. It's almost 6 o'clock when that drink he'd been putting off beckons. The news is depressing, the selection of TV shows is equally depressing, so Sean settles into searching Netflix for a modicum of relaxation.

Actually, there are two or three documentaries that pique his interest. Sleep soon follows. He falls into a deep state of mindless, dreamless sleep but again wakes unexpectedly refreshed.

There is no point sitting by the phone, proverbially speaking, so Sean decides to go through every drawer, cubby, and closet. He's not sure what he's looking for, but it kills time until the long-awaited call finally comes.

"Mr. McCallum, it's Neil Blakely. I just had a long, but not productive conversation with your favorite OPD detective. Polski sure has a bee in his bonnet. He is absolutely convinced you killed Margaret Adams, but he simply can't prove it . . . yet. I asked him for the autopsy reports, but he is playing coy and says it's still ongoing. He did reveal that the victim was dead before she ended up in the water. Any discussion about accidental drowning off the table."

"I'm not sure whether this is good news or bad news," Sean replies.

"Actually, it's a little of each. The good news is that Polski's got basically no evidence against you. Any motive is contrived at best. You know, lover's quarrel gets physical and victim is pushed. Polski has semi-conceded that the trauma was caused by her smacking the concrete with her head. What he has to do is tie you to causation of the fall."

"How did her body get into the pool?" Sean's voice cracks a bit.

"Big unknown. Did someone find the body and push it into the pool? Why? Did the person with whom she was arguing, presumably you, push her, causing her to fall and then panicked and shoved her into the water? Did she fall accidentally and was then pushed into the pool. That's not murder. Tampering with evidence maybe, but certainly not murder. Polski is not letting go. He is convinced you had a role in Margaret's death. I am a bit suspicious of why he is sitting on the autopsy report. He knows something and is trying not to share it with us. He can only do that for a certain, rather limited amount of time before I get an order forcing disclosure." Blakely states very matter-of-factly.

"How long do you want to wait?" Sean is becoming uneasy.

"Until tomorrow afternoon. I am still convinced that there is a piece of information Polski is withholding and he wants to keep it withheld for as long as possible."

"Why?"

"The best reason I can think of is that the information exonerates you and Polski knows it. The longer he can make us think he's got the goods on you, the more likely a deal can be struck."

"Deal?"

"Try to panic you into admitting something." Sean's attorney is confusing him.

"Why should I admit to something I didn't do?" Sean thinks his question sounds reasonable.

"A lot of people crumble under the strain of a police investigation, especially a homicide. They can't take the pressure and will admit to anything to make it go away."

"The deal would have to be pretty good to confess, even to a lesser offense if you didn't commit any crime."

"People are not as strong as you think."

'Ain't that the truth', Sean thinks to himself.

"Counsellor, I don't panic. Do what must be done to force Polski to disclose what he's got. The sooner the better."

"Sounds like I have my marching orders and I agree whole heartedly. There is something gnawing at me. Why is Detective Polski taking this so personal?"

"May I suggest a reason?"

"Please do." Attorney Blakely's curiosity is rising.

"It has nothing to do with the case. It has something to do with his employment. Maybe he was passed over for promotion and needs a big win. Maybe his wife is pushing for that promotion so she can move into a new house or get a new car. It doesn't make sense otherwise. Your thoughts?"

"I must confess that you may have hit the nail on the head. Polski been on the force for a long time and is basically considered a good, clean cop. But he is still only a detective. Might be worth looking into. I'll ask around and see what turns up. Curiouser and curiouser, as my dear mother would say."

"Thanks and keep me posted. Maybe pushing back at Polski is just what the doctor . . . or shall I say pathologist, ordered." Sean chuckles at his joke.

"Agreed. I'll let you know if anything turns up." They disconnect.

CHAPTER TWENTY-SEVEN

Sean feels good about his conversation. He has the utmost confidence that Neil Blakely was a good choice. He decides that he needs to move forward with marshalling his assets and Ryan's assets into a single account in the Cayman Islands. How much can he do by email, fax, and phone? He has already pushed Sean account at Simpson, Tucker to the Grand Cayman account. Now, he needs to create an account in Ryan's name in Grand Cayman. Based on his previous experience, that will require an in-person appearance. Until he can get there, he decides to consolidate some of Ryan's accounts. Make it look like he is fine tuning his portfolio while he is home sick, rather than liquidating it.

Ryan's cell rings. It's Stephen Blackman. Shit. The ringing finally stops, and the notice of message beep tells Sean that he is going to have to deal with this problem sooner rather than later. Quick text saying: "I am in waiting room at my doctor's office. Will call later." He needs to get out of Dodge real soon.

The phone rings again. This time it's Doris.

"Hi ya darling. I'm glad you called. I have been so tied up trying to put out fires at the office I haven't had a minute."

"I just wanted to tell you that I got an A-minus on my term paper. I guess that means I'm ready to start my own B&B, preferably on some island in the Caribbean with you tasting piña coladas to make sure they are perfect." Doris laughs.

"Maybe sooner than you think. As soon as one more conflagration is extinguished, we're off to paradise." Sean sighs. Maybe being with Doris is actually a good thing.

"Sounds great. Any idea of timing. I want to let my boss at the restaurant have time to get a replacement."

"He may get someone else to work the tables, but he'll never replace you." Sean is getting wound up.

"Wow! Maybe I should drive up to Orlando and keep you company until your fire fighting is over."

"Give me a week. If I'm not done by then, fill your gas tank and hit the road."

"Sounds like a plan. Love you. See you soon."

"Love you too. Bye." Sean pushed the red button. *She really makes me feel good.* Now, it's up to Attorney Blakely. Sean reconsiders. It's not too early to have a drink.

The screeching sound of the unit intercom interrupts his momentary euphoria. The image on the security screen sends shivers down Sean's spine: Stephen Blackman—in the flesh. This is definitely not good. He decides that trying to ignore his brother's best friend and lawyer is not a good idea. He pushes the TALK button.

"Hey there, what a surprise. I thought you were on trial or something up in Boston."

"Just buzz me up. We've got to talk." Stephen's voice sounds cold and distant.

Sean pushes the buzzer to admit Stephen. This is not good. A knock on the door quickly follows and the otherwise normally meek attorney almost pushes the door off the hinges.

"Would you like to tell me what the hell this is all about . . . Sean?"

"It may take a while. Would you like a drink?

"Actually, that's not a bad idea. I'll make it."

Is Attorney Blackman being super cautious or is he a picky drinker?

"What would you like, Sean?"

The emphasis on his name unnerves Sean.

"I would like a single malt with a couple of ice cubes. Thanks"

"I figure I know my way around Ryan's condo as well as you do."

Sean rethinks the ice cubes. Stephens voice is below absolute zero.

With practiced efficiency Stephen mixes each a drink and hands a glass of rich amber liquid to Sean.

"Start at the beginning. And no bull shit. I am very good at figuring out if someone is lying."

"Long and short, Ryan came down to South Beach to visit me last week. He said he needed some time off and he wanted to talk with me. I was a bit suspicious but it had been a long time since we talked. He told me all about Margaret's death and how the cops think he had something to do with it. He said he had met with the investigating detective and admitted they'd been together that night, that they had argued but that she had been alive and well when he left. Ryan was rattled. He finally came around to acknowledging that Margaret had stormed out of the house but had tripped and fallen and smacked her head on the patio. But he insisted that he was twenty feet away when she fell and that he had not been aggressive or threatening.

I asked him how she had ended up in the pool. He acted as if he didn't know. Like maybe she crawled and fell in and drowned, although he acted as if he knew she was already dead. I simply said that an autopsy would show whether she died before she was in the pool and left it at that."

"For some strange reason I think you are telling the truth. Please continue." Stephen's voice remains cold.

"Nothing else was said about Margaret. The next day we did some South Beach shopping and then went to a restaurant. As we were leaving, a guy came up to Ryan and shot him. I found out from the Miami cops that the shooter was a local who thought I was having a thing with his wife when he was in prison and mistook Ryan for me. There was nothing I could do for my brother, but I instantly saw the chance to bury my past by assuming Ryan's identity. Basically, that's the whole story except that Ryan is in more trouble than I ever imagined with an obsessed cop on his case."

"Let me get this straight, you decide to become Ryan, bury Sean, get your brother's money, and head for the hills. Am I missing anything?"

"You make it sound a bit more insidious than I would prefer, but basically . . . yes."

"And now you are in trouble because Ryan left a bit of a mess." Stephen is so matter of fact.

"The detective wants to connect me with Margaret's death somehow."

"Assuming that Ryan's version, which is essentially what he told me, is correct, the only crime is tampering with evidence. Hardly a capital offense."

"That's what my lawyer said, except that I can't prove Ryan didn't push or in some way cause Margaret to fall." Sean is trying to make sense.

"True, but an autopsy would show if there were any marks on her body. Bruises or contusions."

"Except Detective Polski won't turn over the report." Sean almost screams.

"Why not? What's his angle?" Stephen's tone is softer.

"Good question. My attorney is doing some behind the scenes digging. He said he can go to court and get an order compelling that we get a copy, but that cop says it's not yet complete. I haven't been charged or even named a person of interest, so by going to court we may force the state attorney to have me charged with murder or manslaughter."

"This is not what I expected. I want to give this some thought. I have a meeting with the FBI tomorrow to try to get them off of your back, I mean Ryan's back. I am going to use the *you can't arrest a dead person* argument."

"There may be a wrinkle in the argument that you should know. It might help, it might not. I closed Sean's account at Simpson, Tucker and transferred the money to my account in the Grand Cayman. There may be some confusion about the date the account was closed but I have backdated a transfer authorization document in the file which predates the shooting."

"You certainly do not make things easy, but you may have given the feds another reason to close the books on this. We need to get the Margaret thing resolved. That bothers me."

"Me too. Look I'm sorry that I used Ryan being shot in such a cavalier fashion, but I only had a few seconds, and the self-preservation instinct took over. If there had been anything I could have done for Ryan, believe me I would have."

"For some reason, I believe you. Ryan always talked about the bond between you. Anyway, what's done is done. I'll call you after meeting with the feds. Thanks for the drink. I gave the bottle to Ryan for Christmas." Stephen rises and quickly walks to the door.

CHAPTER TWENTY-EIGHT

Sean is not sure how he feels about his meeting with Stephen Blackman. On one hand he is relieved that the cat is out of the bag, but on the other he is not sure where his late brother's best friend comes down with the identity switch. There's nothing to do but wait, something at which Sean does not excel. He has a gnawing sense that he has overlooked something. But what? Maybe in the morning he'll hear from Attorney Blakely and by noon Attorney Blackman will have convinced the feds to go chase someone else and leave the grieving brother alone. Fat chance.

Sean is beginning to get really stir crazy. He needs to get out of Ryan's condo, breathe fresh air, be around people. Sean decides to find a small local restaurant and get some real restaurant food for a change. Fortunately, brother Ryan's building is located in an up and coming—formerly down and out—neighborhood. There are several appealing eating and drinking establishments boasting a variety of cuisines. Despite all the temptations, Sean settles for a good old-fashioned burger and beer joint. Much to his surprise, the place is busy as a beehive which allows him to blend in with the crowd. The wait staff is dressed in rainbow emblazoned shirts. Sean feels right at home coming from South Beach. And his burger is fantastic, the beer is served in a chilled mug. No wonder Ryan liked living here. Sean just hopes no one mistakes him for his twin. The patrons are friendly, but distant, which suits Sean just fine.

After a quick walk, Sean returns to the apartment. The message light on Ryan's computer is flashing. Sean quickly boots up the laptop. It's a message from Attorney Blakely.

Please call me first thing in the morning. We need to talk. Polski is a problem . . . to a lot of folks.

Sean re-reads the message. What does it mean that Detective Polski is a problem? And who are the folks to whom he is a problem? Sounds intriguing, but neither good nor bad, and there is absolutely nothing he can do about it until morning.

Sean decides to reply to the email even though his attorney may not read it until tomorrow:

I will call at 9 AM—free all day to meet. Thanks

A hot shower and straight to bed. Just like his mother used to make the boys do after a long day. It actually works provided you don't have about a million things on your mind. It's better than late night TV and there is a chance one might even fall into a deep sleep, albeit for only about four hours.

The morning is hot and humid even for Central Florida. The weather folks say that the temperature will rise to the mid-90s with severe thunderstorms around 4 in the afternoon. Sounds like every day in South Florida. Sean hopes his meeting with Attorney Blakely will be earlier rather than later. Orlando is not a very commuter friendly town. Too many cars, too little parking and too many tourists who have no idea where they are going, coupled with a totally inadequate public transportation system and the world's worst designed roads. It's a total nightmare!

Ryan's cell phone rings. The caller ID indicates it's from his attorney. Impressive since it's only a few minutes after 7. Early bird and all that.

"Good morning, counselor," Sean answers.

"Top of the morning and a hot one it's going to be both literally and figuratively."

"What's cooking?"

"Eggs on the asphalt."

"Enough hot time in the city. I'm all ears." Sean is getting a bit testy.

"I had a chat over a very expensive wine, which I am putting on your bill, with the senior prosecutor in the State Attorney's office. He's a career guy who loves his job, hates politics and is as straight as an arrow. Bottom line, Detective Polski has been on their office radar for over a year. Although his conviction record is fantastic, most are plea deals where it seems evidence has disappeared, been tainted, been withheld . . . you get the picture. Polski will do anything to get a guilty. Seems like the guy has been passed over a lot, whether because of his questionable tactics or because he is considered a jerk, I don't know, nor care."

"Is this good or bad for me?"

"At one level it's not good because the autopsy report is a critical piece of your defense, but it's very good at another level."

"Please explain." Sean is not sure where this is going.

"The prosecutor wants you to be the black widow spider and catch Polski."

"Pray tell me how and what's in it for me?"

"Details will be forthcoming, but basically the Prosecutor's office is going to get the autopsy report directly from the coroner, while we are going to get the report from Polski after securing a court order that he turn it over."

"And compare the two reports."

"Bingo."

"How do I benefit except to get this guy off my case?"

"If the report shows no evidence of foul play, like bruises on the victim's face or arms, and that the victim was dead before she ended up in the pool, the case will be dropped. If it shows she'd been in an altercation, you will be indicted and tried unless we can find another suspect. I think that their case is weak but it's always a crap shoot. Let's hope that the report is clean and that the report we get from Polski and the one the prosecutor's office gets are different, especially in a material way like something that could exonerate you is mysteriously not included in our copy of the report."

"You've accomplished a lot in a little period of time."

"Ryan, time is not our friend. All this has to come down soon before people start asking the prosecutor's office to provide a status report. This is still a death case under investigation."

"What's the plan?"

"I have scheduled a hearing before Magistrate Joan Mayfield for 2 PM. I have prepared, and will send over to the State Attorney's office, a Motion to Compel. The motion will be assigned to my contact who will appear and not object to the report being released forthwith to us. I suspect that Polski will show up but will not be permitted to speak unless the magistrate has a question. I will not mention him in my argument except to say he is the officer in charge of the case. The standard procedure is be to release the report to the investigating detective who in turn will release it to us."

"After he has time to change it."

"Bingo again."

"How will the prosecutor's office get the original autopsy report before it can be changed?'

"As soon as we agree on the strategy, the prosecutor will call the Medical Examiner's office and request the report and send over someone from his office to physically pick it up. I expect it will be in hand before Polski knows about the Motion to Compel. Dollars to donuts, he will pay a visit to the ME's office and ask for the report. Nothing will be mentioned about the prosecutor's copy."

"So, Detective Polski is being set up?"

"I'd rather say he is being given an opportunity to make the right choice. It's up to him."

"Sounds like a solid game plan. Shall I be in court?"

"Yes. It'll give the magistrate a visual. I think that's important. Keep your emotions, including facial expressions, to an absolute minimum."

"Got it, boss. Shall I meet you at your office or at court?"

"I've got several hearings I need to attend this morning, so I'll meet you a few minutes before 2:00 at the court-house, room 7B."

"Great job . . . and thanks." Sean disconnects. He is very pleased, although still cautious. Years in his line of work has taught him not to predict how the judicial process will play out, but at least his attorney seems to be in control."

CHAPTER TWENTY-NINE

Another shower followed by a brisk walk and maybe a cappuccino and a pastry at the boutique coffee shop he saw yesterday. Orlando is a relatively small city in terms of distances, so Sean decides to map out a walking route that will get him to the courthouse by 1:30, allowing time to pass through security and find the right room. Maybe all the pieces are finally falling together. Even the wind has shifted bringing drier and cooler weather to the City Beautiful.

The Orange County Courthouse is a rather plain building as courthouses go, but it is easy to navigate. Security is quick, but thorough and there are electronic announcement boards showing case schedules and rooms. 7B is on the seventh floor. Sean arrives almost twenty minutes early and sees Detective Polski in a heated discussion with a tall, distinguished looking man whom Sean assumes in the prosecutor with whom his attorney had a little chat. He is concentrating so hard that he doesn't even notice that Neil Blakely was seated next to him on the bench.

"They're really going at it." A small smile or maybe a smirk appears on his attorney's face.

"Why is Polski so hot under the collar?"

"The prosecutor's office is intervening in what Polski thinks is his exclusive domain. Control of the evidence. Don't worry, Tom has seen cops come and go and he is not at all intimidated."

"Tom?"

"Tom Morganthaler. He is my contact."

"Gottcha."

The courtroom door opens, and the officer announces that the magistrate is ready. We all file in. The two attorneys each sit at a long table each with a computer monitor, while Polski and Sean each sit in the first row behind the 'bar' that divides the courtroom.

"Hear ye, hear ye, the Honorable Joan Mayfield presiding," the bailiff recites.

"Good afternoon gentlemen." The magistrate's voice is rather gravel-like. "We are here on Mr. Blakely's motion to compel the production of the autopsy report relating to the death of Margaret Adams. The motion recites that Mr. Blakely's client, Mr. Ryan McCallum, is a suspect in her death and that despite several requests, the investigating officer has not yet produced the report. Is that correct?"

"Yes, your Honor," Neil Blakely replies.

"Yes, your Honor, except that the investigating officer Detective Polski says the report is not complete," Tom Morganthaler responds.

"I have a simple solution; Detective Polski is to provide the report to Attorney Blakely before the end of today and the report may be substituted for the final report if there are any changes. Fair enough?"

Both attorneys reply that they are satisfied. Detective Polski is as red as a beet.

"Good . . . next case."

End of hearing. Polski literally storms out of the courtroom. Attorney Morganthaler nods to us and makes a 'I'll call you later' gesture.

Neil Blakely leans over and whispers, "I'll call you when I get the report and hear from the prosecutor."

Sean nods, turns, and walks toward the elevator. He is going to enjoy the walk back to the condominium. Maybe he'll call Doris.

It was after 6 when Attorney Blakely finally called.

"I've got good news and better news, which would you prefer?"

"I'll let you decide." Sean is trying to keep his emotions somewhat under control, which is not easy.

"The autopsy report says that Margaret Adams died as a result of a massive cerebral aneurysm or intracranial aneurysm. She was dead before she hit the ground. The report hypothesizes that she was standing at the edge of the pool when the incident took place, which is why she fell into the pool and also why no water was found in her lungs. Death by natural causes. Also, Morganthaler's copy of the report and my copy are different. The copy I got from Polski includes neither the conclusion that death was from natural causes, nor the medical examiner's hypothesis regard finding the body in the pool."

"Now what?"

"We request for an inquest into cause of death asking the court to declare that Margaret Adams died of natural causes as a result of a brain aneurysm. End of case."

"Wow. When is this hearing going to take place?" Sean is really eager to get this over.

"I am trying to schedule it for the day after tomorrow. Morganthaler will agree to an expedited hearing. I think his office has a surprise for Detective Polski. We won't know when we can schedule a hearing until I speak with the magistrate's clerk to see if she can squeeze us in. Morganthaler will be checking on the coroner's availability. His testimony will be necessary to introduce the real report into evidence."

"What about the changed report?"

"That is in the State Attorney's ballpark although I suspect that the discrepancy will be pointed out to the magistrate."

Attorney Blakely seems very pleased with himself, Sean thinks. As well he should.

"I guess there is nothing for me to do until I hear from you."

"As soon as I get a time for the hearing, I'll let you know."

"Thanks . . . counselor." Sean disconnects. Two days is going to seem like a lifetime, but . . . as Sun Tzu said . . . *Wheels of justice g(r)ind slow but grind fine.*

The phone immediately rings again.

"Sean, it's Stephen Blackman. I just wanted to let you know that I met with the feds, and they are no longer interested in Ryan McCallum."

"That sounds good." Sean is a little unnerved that the FBI was pushing Ryan to get the goods on him. Blackman still makes him feel a little edgy. Maybe that's just his demeanor and his best friend was just killed. "Is there anything for me to do?"

"Nothing. How is the Margaret Adams situation working out?"

"I think that the cops are no longer interested in Ryan either. We have a hearing in a couple of days. It is a coroner's inquest to get her death declared *of natural causes.*"

"When and where is the hearing?"

"I'm not sure yet but probably within the next couple of days."

"I may have to go back to Boston, but I'll check in." The phone goes dead.

He is certainly a hard bird to read, Sean thinks. Blackman seems non plussed by Ryan's death or that Sean has assumed his identity. Cold bastard. Sean starts to whistle '*Off to see the Wizard*' and briskly walks to Ryan's liquor cabinet. Nothing hard, just some wine. Maybe some crackers and cheese. It's been an eventful day. Sean snaps his fingers—tomorrow he will visit Sea World or Universal. It's an Orlando thing.

CHAPTER THIRTY

The ring tone on Ryan's phone is definitely obnoxious, especially this early in the morning.

"Hello," Sean sleepily answers.

"And good morning to you." Neil Blakely sounds entirely too cheerful. "There has been a change in plans."

"Is that a good thing or a not so good thing?"

"For you it's a very good thing but for Detective Polski it looks like a very bad thing."

"Please provide a few more details."

"The State Attorney's office will not oppose a finding that Margaret Adam died of natural causes, which means the end of the investigation and your slate is wiped clean. Tragic circumstance, but a circumstance in which you did not participate, nevertheless."

"Why do I feel you've got something else to say?" Sean is waiting for the other shoe to fall.

"Morganthaler wants to bury Polski and needs your help . . . well at least your testimony."

"About what?" Sean curiosity is peeked.

"Basically he wants to set the stage. How you first approached Polski after hearing of Margaret's death. How you provided him with a signed statement. How he kept dogging you and even trying to intimidate you."

"Okay, I can do that."

"Then Attorney Morganthaler has a couple of other witnesses who have also been treated rather rough shoddily by Polski. Lastly, he will be calling the ME who will testify that the report given to Morganthaler is his report and that it has been completed for three days. The prosecutor will then introduce the altered report which Polski gave us pursuant to the Court's order. Depending how open her honor is to admitting it into evidence, you may have to identify the report that I received from Polski. It will be obvious to Magistrate Mayfield that the two reports are not the same and that material portions of the authentic report have been deleted. There's a little hearsay issue since I actually received the report, but inquests are a bit looser on the admission of evidence than a jury trial. If it comes to that, I will be able to testify as to the chain of possession from Polski, to me, and then to you if the matter gets to the grand jury."

"Sounds good." Sean is pleased.

"You will need to meet with Morganthaler's assistant to go over your testimony. It shouldn't take more than an hour, at most."

"Then what?"

"Then we have the inquest hearing tomorrow I will ask the judge to enter findings that the death of Margaret Adams was from natural causes. And then the fireworks."

"I don't like the sound of that."

"Not to worry. Nothing to impact you. The State Attorney's office will ask that a criminal complaint be issued for evidence tampering against Polski, that, until further order, he be suspended from the Orlando Police Department, that he is a flight risk, that a substantial bond be set, and that he be ordered to wear a monitor and have no contact with any one remotely connected to the case.

The Court may also find him in contempt both regarding the representation that the report was not complete and disregarding her order to turn over the actual report."

"Holy shit. That's a lot coming down on the poor bastard all at once and without notice."

"Ryan, don't waste another minute concerning yourself with former Detective Michael Polski. He is a bad apple. He has subverted the entire criminal process. I suspect that this is the tip of the iceberg. Morganthaler's team is going to have to review every case Polski handled for the last five years, at least."

"What should I do?"

"I have arranged for you to meet with an assistant prosecutor at 11 AM at my office this morning. I thought I should be around to make sure there are no problems."

"Problems?"

"Until the magistrate issues her order, it's not totally over."

"You mean until the fat lady sings?" Sean chuckles.

"Magistrate Mayfield would be a bit miffed if she heard that she is being referred to as the 'fat lady'." Attorney Blakely starts to laugh. "See you in a couple of hours."

"Well done. Well done." Sean breathes an audible sigh of relief.

After ringing off with Attorney Blakely, Sean is tempted to call Doris but decides to wait until the proceeding is all over. No loose ends.

After a super-hot shower, breakfast beckons. The coffee shop he frequented yesterday is just what the doctor ordered, figuratively speaking.

Sean arrives at his attorney's office almost twenty minutes early. The waiting room is empty except for a twenty-something young lawyer who looks like the runner-up in the last Miss America pageant.

Reality hits when Neil Blakely enters and says, "Ryan, I'd like you to meet assistant State Attorney Deborah Weber. She will be prepping you for tomorrow's hearing. You guys go into the conference room. If you need me, I'll be in my office trying to catch up on paperwork."

Attorney Blakely's receptionist opens the door. "There is fresh coffee and cold bottled water on the sideboard. If there is anything else you'd like, just let me know."

Ever the gentleman, Sean holds Attorney Weber's seat.

"Thank you and I thought chivalry was dead." Her voice is deep and husky but sultry.

Suddenly, her phone rings.

"Excuse me," she says to Sean. "Yes sir, I'm here with Mr. McCallum now." There is a momentary pause. "I'll get him. Please hold."

Again to Sean, "It's my boss. He wants to conference in Attorney Blakely."

"I'll get him," Sean replies. He opens the door and quickly reappears with Neil Blakely in tow.

"We are all here on speaker," Deborah Weber announces.

"Neil, I want to go to plan B," State Attorney Morganthaler announces. "Seems like Detective Polski is taking the inquest personally. He wants to say his two cents worth. If he wants to open the door, let him."

"Tom, let me explain this to Mr. McCallum so that he understands what you are planning."

"Good idea."

"If Detective Polski is crazy enough to want to testify, who better to identify the fake autopsy report? Your testimony was a bit sketchy and depended on the magistrate being flexible. This way, Polski will ID the autopsy report he gave us, and the medical examiner will testify that the second document is the real record and that it was prepared three days ago and given to Polski. Case closed. Do I have that right, Tom?"

"Right as rain. I don't care if Polski talks about his suspicions about Mr. McCallum, the report speaks for itself . . . death by natural causes. Also Michael Polski will be looking down the barrel of Magistrate Mayfield's judicial cannon. He will have admitted changing a document, violating the Court order to turn over the report, lying to the Court that the report was not final and probably several more things I will think up before tomorrow. Mr. McCallum, your testimony is no longer needed, but Attorney Weber's presence in the office is. Bye all."

"As my favorite cartoon character once said, 'That's all folks.' See you all tomorrow at 2 in room 7A." Attorney Blakely rises, nods, and leaves.

"It was a pleasure meeting you Mr. McCallum," Deborah Weber says with an enchanting smile.

"All too short." Sean is enchanted by the young prosecutor.

"There's always tomorrow."

"And tomorrow and tomorrow," Sean quips.

They both rise and leave.

CHAPTER THIRTY-ONE

Hear ye, hear ye, the Honorable Joan Mayfield presiding," the bailiff recites.

"Good afternoon. Please state your name for the stenographer."

Tom Morganthaler nods to Sean's attorney.

"Your Honor, my name is Neil Blakely and I represent Ryan McCallum who is standing to my right." Blakely nods back to the State Attorney.

"Good afternoon Your Honor. My name is Thomas Morganthaler. Joining me is assistant State Attorney Deborah Weber and Orlando police detective Michael Polski."

"Thank you. This is a medical examiner inquest hearing. Is someone from the ME's office here?"

"Yes, Your Honor. My name is Dr. Victor Wasserman, and I am the chief medical examiner for Orange County."

"Are you going to testify this afternoon, Dr. Wasserman?"

"Yes, Your Honor."

"Is anyone else going to testify?"

Polski is starring at Attorney Morganthaler.

"Yes Your Honor, Detective Polski wishes to testify, as well."

"Is Detective Polski the lead investigative officer?"

"Yes he is, Your Honor."

"Any other witnesses?"

Blakely and Morganthaler answer in unison, "No, Your Honor."

"Will the witnesses rise, and will the clerk administer the oath?"

"Do you both affirm to tell the truth, the whole truth and nothing but the truth?"

Both men answer in the affirmative.

"The purpose of this hearing is to ascertain, if possible, the cause of death of Margaret Adams. This is not an adversarial preceding in that respect. I simply want facts, not conjectures or theories. Understood?"

Everyone replies that they understand.

"Mr. Morganthaler, your witness, please."

"The State calls Michael Polski."

Polski almost flies toward the witness stand.

Attorney Morganthaler slowly approaches Detective Polski, who is twitching in his seat.

"Please tell the Court your full name and your occupation?"

"My name is Michael Francis Polski. I am a detective with the Orlando Police Department."

"How long have you been employed by the OPD?"

"I have been employed for twenty-one years, the last five years as a detective in the violent crimes division."

"Were you the chief investigator in the death of Margaret Adams?" Morganthaler is very controlled.

"I still am the chief investigator," Polski retorts.

"In your role as chief investigator, did you receive an autopsy report from the Medical Examiner's office?"

"Yes."

"When did you receive the report?"

"I received an interim report three days ago."

"You were in Court two days ago when her Honor ordered you to turn over the report to Attorney Blakely, correct?"

"Yes."

"Did you do so?"

"As ordered, I turned over the report to Attorney Blakely before the end of the day."

"Is this a copy of the report you gave Attorney Blakely? Please review it carefully."

Detective Polski reads the report. While doing so, he continually nods.

"Yes, this is a copy of the report I sent Attorney Blakely."

"Is it also a copy of the report you received from the ME's office?"

"Yes."

"Your Honor, may I introduce this report as Exhibit A?"

"Without objection, the report is so introduced."

Attorney Morganthaler hands the document to the clerk who stamps the report and returns it to Morganthaler.

"Counsellor, may I see the document?" Magistrate Maybury asks.

The State Attorney hands the report to the magistrate who reads it carefully.

"You may continue Mr. Morganthaler," Magistrate Maybury says after she has reviewed the entire report.

"I have no further questions," he replies.

Detective Polski stands up and begins to virtually shout, "I have a lot more to say about this case, Your Honor. A lot."

"Mr. Polski, please lower your voice and sit down and listen. This hearing is only to determine the cause of death. If the Court concludes that the cause of death was natural, that is the end. If the Court concludes that it is unable to determine the cause of death or finds that death was caused by a person or persons unknown, then we will go to the next level, and I am sure that the prosecutor's office will solicit everything you uncovered in your investigation. But this is neither the time nor place, so unless Mr. Blakely has any questions you are dismissed and may step down."

"I have no questions, Your Honor," Neil Blakely replies.

"Mr. Morganthaler . . . you next witness, please."

"The State calls Dr. Victor Wasserman to the stand."

Despite a shock of white hair, Dr. Wasserman briskly walks up to the witness stand.

"Please tell the Court your name and occupation."

"My name is Victor Wasserman, and I am the chief medical examiner for Orange County."

"How long have you been employed by Orange County?"

"My actual employer is the Sunshine Medical Center where I am head of pathology. I also serve as medical examiner for Orange County in which Orlando is located."

"What is your educational background?"

"Mr. Morganthaler, Dr. Wasserman is well known to the Court and assuming Attorney Blakely has no objections, I am certifying him as an expert in the field of pathology."

"No objection, Your Honor." Blakely keeps it short and sweet.

"Please continue, Mr. Morganthaler." Magistrate Maybury wants to hear Dr. Wasserman's opinion.

"Dr. Wasserman, I would like you to identify this document."

"This is my report of findings after completing an autopsy on Margaret Adams."

"Your Honor, I would like to introduce the report as Exhibit B."

"Without objection, I will admit the document as Exhibit B."

"No objection," Attorney Blakely inserts.

"I have a simple question," Magistrate Maybury says. "Why do we need both Exhibit A and Exhibit B?"

"If the Court bares me just a little leeway, it will become obvious."

"A few minutes Counsellor," Magistrate Maybury replies.

"Dr. Wasserman, I would like to show you what has been marked as Exhibit A and ask if you have ever seen this document before." Prosecutor Morganthaler hands him Exhibit A.

"This report is a redacted or modified version of my report. May I have my report and I will explain?

The clerk hands the ME Exhibit B.

Dr. Wasserman continues, "my report is very clear. It states the cause of death based on my findings and conclusions. The entire paragraph is missing from the Detective Polski's version. Also the heading which says *INTERIM* has been added. I do not prepare interim reports."

"Dr. Wasserman, when did you complete your report?"

"I reviewed the report four days ago and signed it. I sent a copy to our records department in electronic form and to Detective Polski as well."

"Is it fair to say that Detective Polski had the final report in his possession three days ago."

"The final and only report," Dr. Wasserman retorts.

"Attorney Morganthaler, is this going where I think it's going?" Magistrate Maybury is clearly unhappy.

"In part, Your Honor. I want to go through Dr. Wasserman's autopsy report and ask him for his opinion regarding cause of death. Then, I suggest a bench conference to decide where we go from here."

"Bench conference, now." Both Blakely and Morganthaler hustle over to the front of the bench.

"I have heard enough about Detective Polski to hold him in contempt and charge him with evidence tampering. Is there anything else?"

"Our office has been investigating Mr. Polski for some time and this may be only the latest incident."

"This is not good. I want to keep this hearing clean on the record. Dr. Wasserman's opinion goes to the case in chief. There is nothing else that needs to be introduced concerning Mr. Polski. I am going to find him guilty of contempt and hold him on probably cause." The magistrate signals to her head bailiff, who joins the others. "Buddy, I assume you've put one and one together." Buddy is as big as a house and looks strong enough to lift one.

He nods. "A cell is waiting downstairs. I have two men just outside the rear courtroom door, one at your lobby door and me."

"I will make a finding, then take a five-minute recess. Is that enough time?"

"Ma'am, he's armed but not stupid. I will slightly adjust my position to put myself behind him and the minute you rise to make your finding, I will put him into a friendly bear hug."

"Your Honor, may I give Attorney Weber a fake assignment, and get her out of the courtroom," State Attorney Morganthaler asks.

"I will do one better. Attorney Weber, we are a bit short handed this afternoon. I hate to ask but would go down to my clerk's office and bring back my calendar file?"

"Of course, Your Honor." She gets up, moves away from Polski, and walks out the rear courtroom door.

"Back to business," Magistrate Maybury whispers. "Dr. Wasserman, Detective Polski, I'm sorry for the delay. Some other court business has just come up and we needed to discuss scheduling."

Sean is dumbfounded by all this posturing. He just wants to get the Magistrate to say Margaret's death was from natural causes, finish packing, call Doris, and split.

CHAPTER THIRTY-TWO

Befo efore continuing with Dr. Wasserman's testimony, the Court has a housekeeping matter to attend to. Michael Francis Polski, please rise."

If nervousness gives off a unique smell, the courtroom is filled with the odor. Polski slowly rises to his feet and within a nano second he is fully embraced by the giant bailiff. Morganthaler reached under Polski's suit coat and removes both his badge and issue automatic. He then pats down the about to be former cop, retrieving a diminutive pistol from an ankle holster.

"Mr. Polski, the Court finds that you willfully, knowingly, and with intent to deceive the Court violated the Order requiring you to provide Attorney Blakely with a copy of Dr. Wasserman's report. Further, the Court finds that you willfully, knowingly, and with intent to undermine the judicial process redacted, changed, and modified said report, lied to the Court regarding when you came into possession of the report, and further, that you falsified the report as an interim report. The Court sentences you to serve ninety days for contempt commencing forthwith and to be bound over to the grand jury for evidence tampering.

Is that sufficient time, Mr. Morganthaler for you to get the rest of your ducks in a row?"

"Yes, Your Honor," he replies.

Polski begins to squirm but against the bailiff, his efforts are useless. Handcuffs are applied by one of the officers from outside and Polski is marched out the side door into the bowels of the courthouse.

Sean is agape. This is more like a movie than the real thing, but he quickly realizes he still needs the Court's decision of death by natural causes. In his world this kind of drama would never have happened. His world was black and white. His brother's world is filled with nuance, innuendo, and game playing. However, there is nothing Sean can do. He is stuck in Ryan's world by his own choice. His only hope is to escape-far, far away.

"The Court will take a five-minute recess. You may use the jury room next door. I'll have coffee and cold water brought up right away." Magistrate Maybury bangs her gavel.

The only sound is the scraping of chairs on the floor.

CHAPTER THIRTY-THREE

The hearing begins in precisely five minutes. Dr. Wasserman returns to the witness box.

"Dr. Wasserman, the Court has qualified you as an expert so you can express opinions as well as report facts. Do you have an opinion of cause of death of Margaret Adams and upon what facts do you base your opinion?"

"Simply said, I examined the deceased shortly after death. The lead detective, Mr. Polski, was very insistent that I be extra thorough. He said he had strong suspicions of foul play. I performed the autopsy bearing in mind the possibility of physical trauma. I only found a small contusion on the side of her head which presented traces of concrete consistent with hitting one's head on the pool deck. To verify my findings, I personally examined the scene, removed concrete scrapings, and compared them to the particles found in the wound area. They matched but had nothing to do with cause of death. The decedent experienced a cerebral, or brain aneurysm, which is a weakened or thin spot on an artery in the brain that balloons and fills with blood. The aneurysm can put pressure on the nerves or brain tissue. In this case the balloon burst. She died instantly."

"Was she dead before her head came in contact with the pool?" Morganthaler asks.

"Margaret Adams was dead before her head struck the concrete. The pool had nothing to do with her death. By way of a brief explanation, brain aneurysms can occur in anyone and at any age. They are most common in adults between the ages of 30 and 60 and are more common in women than in men. Margaret Adams was a ticking time bomb. The decedent could have experienced the aneurysm at any time and in any place."

"Did she die of natural causes?" Attorney Morganthaler wants to make sure the "I's" are dotted and the "T's" are crossed.

"Without equivocation, it is my opinion Margaret Adams died of natural causes."

"Thank you Dr. Wasserman." The State Attorney returns to his seat.

"Any questions, Mr. Blakely?"
"None, Your Honor."

"I declare this hearing over. Give me a few minutes to prepare my findings and draft a brief order. The Court will stand in recess for five minutes and the jury room is still available."

"All rise," Buddy the behemoth bailiff says.

"This has been an amazing day," Sean sputters. "Unbelievably amazing."

Tom Morganthaler and Neil Blakely shake hands. Suddenly, the rear doors open. Deborah Weber, totally clueless of what has been happening walks in. "I have her calendar. At least I think so. What's going on?"

"We are waiting for the court to announces her finding and order."

"I think I missed something."

"Nah . . . same old . . . same old." I think Attorney Morganthaler likes teasing his young, and very pretty associate.

Sean's excitement at finally getting out from under the strain translates into a quick trip to the restroom. The group reassembles in the courtroom as the magistrate enters.

"Let's make this quick. Please be seated. I notice that we are joined by a gentleman in the back. This is a closed hearing, sir."

"Good afternoon, Your Honor. My name is Stephen Blackman, and I am Ryan McCallum's personal attorney, as well as his close friend."

Sean has no idea what Blackman is up to. When the magistrate moves eye contact from Attorney Blackman to him, he decides he had better be cool. He simply nods, which seems to suffice.

"Let us continue shall we? Would Ryan McCallum please rise?"

Suddenly, there is a commotion in the back of the courtroom.

"What is the meaning of this Attorney Blackman?"

"Your Honor if I may have two minutes. I will file an appearance on behalf of Ryan McCallum if that helps."

"Whether it helps or not is not really important. It will make the record complete."

Stephen Blackman opens his briefcase and withdraws a paper.

"You come prepared," Magistrate Maybury says somewhat sarcastically.

The courtroom doors open and in enters Ryan McCallum, arm in a sling, flanked by Agents Tanner and Dylan, each holding their FBI identification for the bailiff to see.

"They're good, Your Honor," Buddy the bailiff says after examining their credentials. "They've got a warrant for the arrest of Sean McCallum for bank fraud, wire fraud, money laundering and a whole lot more."

"Who is Sean McCallum?"

"May I, Your Honor?" Attorney Blackman asks.

"Please do, counsellor. Take as much time as you like but stay on point."

"Sean and Ryan McCallum are identical twins. Ryan was my college school roommate and we've been close friends ever since. Eight days ago I got a call from Agent Tanner, whose office had been interviewing Ryan in connection with his brother Sean. He told me that Sean had been shot in South Beach. I called, then texted Ryan's number to tell him. Long story short, Ryan and Sean were together in Miami when an acquaintance of Sean's approached the two and shot Ryan, mistaking him for Sean.

Sean immediately seized the opportunity and switched identification with his twin and thus assumed the persona of Ryan. I reached out several times to the new Ryan who feigned illness and couldn't talk. I was still trying to resolve Ryan's interaction with the FBI and agreed to meet Agents Tanner and Dylan. Since Sean was dead, their investigation was moot. I also received a call from a nurse at Mercy Hospital in Miami who said that her patient, one Sean

McCallum, kept claiming that there was a mix up in identification and that I could straighten it out. I flew to Miami
and found Ryan, wounded but very much alive. I had him
transferred to a facility in Orlando and then visited Sean at
Ryan's apartment and confronted him. He was contrite and
under the impression that Ryan had been killed and that
this was an opportunity for him to start over. I then met
with Agents Tanner and Dylan and explained the entire
scenario. And here we are."

"That was reasonably clear . . . under the circumstances. The good news is that nothing you have said
changes my finding or my order except to whom it is
directed." The magistrate turns her attention to the two
FBI agents. "My bailiff said you have a warrant for Sean
McCallum's arrest. Is that correct?"

"Yes, Your Honor the pair answer together."

Her attention is now directed at Sean who is pale as a
ghost and quiet as a mouse. "Are you Sean McCallum?"

"Yes ma'am."

"You heard Mr. Blackman' presentation, correct?"

"Yes, Your Honor."

"Is there anything you want to add?"

"No, Your Honor."

"Agents, please serve the warrant and remove Mr.
McCallum."

Sean holds out his hands, awaiting handcuffs. Agent
Tanner steers Sean from the courtroom. The door closes.

"Mr. Ryan McCallum, please come forward. Mr.
Blackman, please accompany him. After reviewing
the coroner's report and hearing the testimony of Dr.
Wasserman I find that Margaret Adams died of natural
causes and that no further inquiry into the circumstances

thereof will be permitted. Good luck and a speedy recovery, Mr. McCallum. Court is adjourned."

Also by D.G. Stern

The Adventures of Upton Charles—Dog Detective
Disappearing Diamonds
Something Fishy
Winter Wonderland
Lost Loot
Ship Shape
Tip Top
Picture Perfect
Time Tale
Missing Map
Super Scary

And coming soon
Double Trouble

Thomas Ballard Mysteries
Stabbing Along the Straightaway
Chaos at the Concourse
Panic in the Pits
Critical Corner
Action at the Auction
Francis
Francis the Firehouse Mouse
Francis at the Farm
Francis at the Beach
Francis at the Ranch
Also
Golf a la Carte
The Loneliest Tree
25 Days of a Tropical Christmas
Hot Tea . . . Cold Case
There's Always Tomorrow
Sophie the Skunk
Fudge Fatale

Visit us on the web at:
www.neptunepress.org